**If word spread that he was actively seeking a wife, half of Dhalkur's aristocratic families would push forward their daughters and the other half would argue their merits—a sure recipe for dissension.**

"I expect the best service. Discreet. Professional. Exceptional."

"And you'll have it. Believe me, Your Majesty, we are committed one hundred percent to meeting your requirements, whatever you desire."

A tingle of static sparked at his nape and raced down his backbone.

*Whatever you desire.*

It reminded him forcefully of what he'd desired the night they met. A desire that was unsatisfied because of the urgent news that had come out of Dhalkur, making an immediate return home necessary.

Why had Rosanna Maclain chosen that particular word?

Was it a Freudian slip? Proof that she too still felt the attraction between them?

Growing up near the beach, **Annie West** spent lots of time observing tall, burnished lifeguards—early research! Now she spends her days fantasizing about gorgeous men and their love lives. Annie has been a reader all her life. She also loves travel, long walks, good company and great food. You can contact her at annie@annie-west.com or via PO Box 1041, Warners Bay, NSW 2282, Australia.

### Books by Annie West

### Harlequin Presents

*The Sheikh's Marriage Proclamation*
*A Consequence Made in Greece*
*The Innocent's Protector in Paradise*
*One Night with Her Forgotten Husband*

### *Royal Scandals*

*Pregnant with His Majesty's Heir*
*Claiming His Virgin Princess*

Visit the Author Profile page
at Harlequin.com for more titles.

# Annie West

---

## THE DESERT KING MEETS HIS MATCH

**HARLEQUIN**
PRESENTS

**H HARLEQUIN®**
# PRESENTS™

Recycling programs for this product may not exist in your area.

ISBN-13: 978-1-335-73867-7

The Desert King Meets His Match

Copyright © 2022 by Annie West

For questions and comments about the quality of this book, please contact us at CustomerService@Harlequin.com.

Harlequin Enterprises ULC
22 Adelaide St. West, 41st Floor
Toronto, Ontario M5H 4E3, Canada
www.Harlequin.com

**Printed in U.S.A.**

# THE DESERT KING MEETS HIS MATCH

This is for all those who like a book to sweep them away to another world.

It's especially for those of you who read *The Sheikh's Marriage Proclamation* and wondered what happened to Tara's cousin, Salim.

I always intended to write his story but your many queries about him spurred me on!

I hope you love this book as much as I do.

# PROLOGUE

'SOMEONE SHOULD OUTLAW the playing of bagpipes indoors.'

The woman on the terrace swung around at his words, the dark waves of her hair swirling invitingly about her shoulders.

Their eyes met and Salim's pulse gave a thud of satisfaction as he felt again that spark of heat.

Indoors the sensation had been muted, for he'd seen her only at a distance. Yet whenever their gazes collided, or he felt her watching him, awareness had prickled between his shoulder blades.

Her lips curved into a wry half-smile that appealed far more than the beaming grins of the socialites he'd fended off inside. 'You're not a fan?'

Salim moved nearer to where she stood, illuminated by flambeaux set on the edge of the lawn. Behind her stretched a silvery loch and beyond that a dark mountain then the vastness of a Scottish summer evening.

Unlike the other female guests, she didn't wear an evening dress but a tuxedo, tailored to fit her curves and long legs. Enticingly long legs. Yet even in basic black she stood out. And not just because of the glittering silver top visible between her satin lapels.

'I wouldn't say that,' he murmured. 'Bagpipes can be quite stirring in the right circumstances.'

He was fascinated to discover a stirring of his own. A physical response to her closeness, low in his body.

It intrigued him. This woman wasn't precisely beautiful, yet she was…alluring.

More, something about her made his inner self whisper a word that sounded remarkably like *Mine*.

That was unusual enough to secure his attention.

Salim was a modern man who dealt in concrete reality, proven facts and double-checked figures. Yet he had a healthy respect for his instincts. They'd saved him more than once in the past. He listened to them now.

Her smile widened and Salim felt it like the slow spread of dawn heat warming the earth after a chill desert night. 'Perhaps you can put in a request for the piper to wake you at dawn. But I doubt it will make you popular with the other guests at the castle.'

The sound of her throaty chuckle sent a ripple of arousal skidding down his spine and straight to his groin.

Salim's brows twitched together. It was one thing to recognise his body's reaction to an attractive woman. It was another to feel arousal like an unbroken horse, stampeding straight through him, galloping out of control.

Perhaps on reflection this wasn't such a good idea.

As he thought it, she half turned away, as if to admire the glen in the fading light. Giving him a reason to end the conversation and return to the party.

As if she weren't interested in him, despite the looks she'd sent his way.

Suddenly, retreating wasn't an option.

Because what else could it be, other than retreat?

As if on cue, Salim heard the French doors open behind him, and the measured steps of the waiter to whom he'd given his order.

'Madam? Sir?' He proffered a silver tray with two champagne flutes.

Salim lifted both glasses and nodded his thanks. As the waiter disappeared he offered one to his companion.

She'd turned towards him again, frowning up under dark eyebrows. Now he was near enough he discovered her eyes were a clear, dark grey. Like the pewter of the loch behind her, or the silvery curve of his ceremonial scimitar.

'You ordered these?'

Her words were sharp like a blade too. Yet Salim read not temper in her eyes but a shadow of something unexpected in this elegant, self-contained woman. Nerves.

Was she, too, wary of this attraction?

'I did. I saw you leave and the idea of quiet conversation seemed infinitely more appealing than the crush inside.' He paused. 'But if you'd prefer solitude...'

'No!' The swift denial reassured. As did the self-aware twitch of her mobile mouth, as if she couldn't find it in herself to pretend. 'Thank you. A drink would be lovely.'

Rosanna didn't do casual flings.

She didn't kiss total strangers.

So how did she come to be plastered against this handsome stranger, her heart thundering in her chest, trying to get still closer to all that luxurious masculine heat?

Even with one strong arm lashed around her waist, his other hand supporting the back of her head as he delved deep into her mouth, she didn't feel close enough.

Even with their tongues tangling, their breathing laboured, heat searing everywhere they touched, she wanted more. So much more.

Rosanna clutched his shoulders with needy hands. She arched, pressing her breasts up against that hard chest, and heard a soft sound, like a growl of approval in the back of his throat, that sent excitement skating through her.

She'd never, in all her twenty-six years, been kissed like this. Or responded so. Such desperate hunger was new and exhilarating.

Fleetingly Phil came to mind. But her brain instantly shied away.

Instead came flashes from tonight.

This man's casual good humour.

The teasing dark gleam of his eyes as they chatted about everything and nothing while inside the other guests partied. The sound of his cut-glass consonants melded with a lilting undercurrent that turned his voice into flagrant temptation.

The way he *listened* to her, even as his eyes dared her to live in the moment.

When had a man ever seduced her with his humour and insight? With wit and charm and that dark, sizzling *something* that reached out and curled around her insides, tugging, tugging, tugging at her until she'd given in and moved closer.

That first touch, hand to hand, that had sent electricity arcing to her breasts and lower, to the place between her legs that pulsed with blatant hunger.

She would have drawn back then, scared by the sudden conflagration inside her. Except she'd seen him frown as if he hadn't expected this full-on slam of need either.

Her hand had somehow drifted to his chest and he'd lifted it from there to his mouth. Her knees had loosened at the sight and feel of his lips on her skin and he'd gathered her close.

Rosanna tilted her head, eagerly shifting against him until he slid his hand down through her hair, past her shoulder and under the lapel of her jacket. Long fingers brushed the spangled fabric of her top, so incredibly slowly she couldn't tell if he gave her time to object or wanted to torture her with longing.

Finally, in desperation, she covered his hand with hers and slid it down to cover her breast.

Lights spun behind her closed eyelids as he cupped her there. His thumb brushed her peaking nipple and she shuddered, clutching at him. Then he squeezed gently and everything inside melted as darts of fire rayed out from his touch. Her desperate gasp tasted of him, champagne, exotic spice and sensuality.

Rosanna gave thanks to the overzealous maid who had offered to launder her blouse and accidentally scooped up her bra while Rosanna showered. The feel of his hard, gentle, capable hand massaging her braless breast through a thin layer of fabric was bliss.

He gathered her closer. She felt the rigidity in his tall frame and the hard shaft of arousal now pressed against her belly.

Heat poured through her. Her flesh prickled. She wanted to be skin to skin against him. A tiny part of her brain registered surprise but she didn't care.

Rosanna's hand went to the soft silk of his formal bow tie and—

'Excuse me, sir.'

They froze. She felt her companion's fingers tighten

reflexively and even that felt good. So good her inner muscles clenched needily.

For one heartbeat, two, neither moved. Then he raised his head. For a moment she felt his breath as a caress across her face. Dark eyes glittered down at her with a promise that weakened something fundamental inside her.

How eagerly Rosanna wanted to accept that promise.

Then he straightened and tucked her in against his shoulder, as if to protect her from the view of the man behind him.

'Yes? What is it?'

'I'm sorry, but there's a call. It's important or I wouldn't have—'

Her companion breathed out, a long exhale that pushed his wide chest against her.

'It's okay, Taqi. I understand.' Another slow breath. 'I'll be there in a moment.'

Rosanna didn't hear the man's footsteps as he left because her pulse was thrumming in her ears.

But he must have gone because suddenly cool air wafted around her. Her companion's hand slid from her breast and she had to stifle a cry of protest as he stepped back, holding her upper arms as if he realised how weak-kneed she felt.

'My apologies,' he murmured and this time that indefinable accent was much stronger.

Rosanna looked into ebony eyes and silently nodded. Was he apologising for the interruption or for getting so carried away in such a public place? They were lucky it was someone he knew, someone apparently discreet, who'd found them.

Yet as she stood there, trying to catch her breath, it wasn't regret she felt, except at the interruption. She'd fallen headlong into a tsunami of desire and it had been the single most exciting event of her life.

Which said an awful lot about her life up until now!

She watched his Adam's apple move jerkily in his throat and felt a burst of relief seeing proof that he too struggled to come back to reality.

'I have to go. It must be important for Taqi to search me out.'

She nodded. 'I understand.'

Still he didn't move, just stood, looking down at her from dark, unreadable eyes. Then he inclined his head. 'Thank you.'

A second later she stood alone as he strode with loose-limbed grace back towards the party.

Rosanna watched him go, hand to her throat as if to keep in her fast-beating heart that had risen there.

She moved away to the dark corner at the end of the terrace, waiting till her breathing returned to normal and the fireworks he'd set off in her body stopped detonating.

Rosanna couldn't quite believe what had happened. She'd never felt such a visceral response to any man, even Phil, whom she'd once planned to marry! Such combustible passion was outside her experience. The realisation should shock her. Yet all Rosanna felt was a sense of inevitability, as if it were utterly natural for a woman who never did one-night stands and had learned to think twice about trusting men to respond this way to a stranger.

And to feel bereft at his departure.

She smoothed down her hair and straightened her jacket, doing up the buttons that had come undone during their embrace. Then she settled on a nearby stone seat, waiting for his return.

He didn't come.

Not long afterwards the doors opened and guests spilled out. For half an hour everyone stood on the terrace, watching an impressive firework display in honour of the laird and his new bride. Tonight was part of a series of celebrations to mark their recent marriage.

But to Rosanna the pyrotechnics were a distraction. In their lurid light she moved through the crowd looking for a particular dark head and broad shoulders. Her fingertips tingled at the memory of his sculpted head and soft, short hair beneath her touch.

But he'd gone.

And she didn't even know his name.

# CHAPTER ONE

'BUT, MARIAN, I'M not ready for this!'

'Of course you are. You're a recruitment expert, aren't you? This is just another recruitment job.'

'*Just* another job?' Rosanna's eyebrows rose as she stared, unseeing, through the huge window that gave out over her aunt's lovely Chelsea garden. 'Surely even by your standards, this isn't just any other job.'

There was a pause on the line and Rosanna imagined her diminutive aunt leaning back in her hospital bed and setting her mouth in a firm line.

'All right. It's not average, even by my standards.'

Which was saying something as Marian Best was known as exactly that, the best in the business. That was how she commanded such high commissions and could afford this gracious house in one of London's most expensive suburbs.

Rosanna breathed a sigh of relief at the acknowledgement that she wasn't stressing over nothing. She was used to working in a high-pressure environment with tight deadlines and sometimes unreasonable demands, but this was way out of the ordinary.

'I can't imagine anyone describing this contract as average. Not when the client is so incredibly high profile—'

'Which is something we don't discuss in public,' her aunt said crisply, as if fearing a hospital orderly or a nurse passing her room might overhear.

Rosanna drew herself up straighter. 'It's okay, Marian. You can count on me to be completely discreet.'

That at least was something she *could* promise. Absolute confidentiality was second nature to her given her previous work as a corporate headhunter. She'd found the right people for jobs that were often sensitive or high profile and absolute discretion was essential.

It was the rest of this task she wondered about.

'I know, Rose. And I can't tell you how grateful I am to have you on board for this.'

Rosanna heard her aunt's voice soften and realised it was concern that had sharpened it earlier.

She was probably as worried as Rosanna about her new-to-the-business niece handling such an extraordinary job. But there was no other choice. Marian's business was very, very exclusive and discreet. So exclusive and discreet it consisted of her and her part-time secretary. And now Rosanna, still learning the ropes. But this was a commission that couldn't be passed up.

And if it didn't work out…

Rosanna shivered and clutched the phone tighter. It wasn't just her reputation and career that would be at risk if she failed, but her aunt's business.

If she failed and their powerful client was displeased, a few dismissive words from him to other, potential clients could wreak destruction.

She drew a careful breath, working to slow her pulse.

'I'll do whatever you want, Marian, but I'll need guidance.'

Was that a sigh of relief from the other end of the line?

Rosanna wished she could sit with her aunt while she

waited for surgery but Marian had insisted there was no time to waste. She'd vetoed a hospital visit and ordered her straight to Chelsea and her home office.

'Of course, and I'll be here, on the other end of the line.' There was a pause. 'Remember everything I've taught you, and that I wouldn't have brought you in to join me if I didn't have faith in you.'

Before Rosanna could thank her for that vote of confidence, Marian went on. 'The stakes may be higher in this case, given the remarkably high profile of our client, but the principles are the same. Now, make a note. These are the files I want you to load to your laptop…'

Twenty minutes later the list of instructions had grown but that was good. Because having specific tasks to do meant there was no time to fret. Until Marian mentioned one last thing.

'The car will collect you at ten o'clock this morning from my front door.'

'Ten?' Rosanna stared at the time, calculating how long it would take her to race to her tiny flat and pack.

'Precisely. So don't dawdle. And good luck.'

Rosanna would need all the luck she could get. For the first time she'd take the lead role in her aunt's phenomenally successful matchmaking business.

If that wasn't tough enough, her first solo job was to find the perfect bride for a sheikh.

A royal sheikh!

It was a long, long way from working in corporate Sydney. Or even helping Marian with her discreet research.

After Phil's duplicity Rosanna's world had fallen apart. Marian's offer of work in Britain had been a lifeline, one she'd grabbed with both hands to escape the gossip and sidelong looks at home. Even her family's sympathy and outrage had felt like a burden.

But she'd only worked in her aunt's firm a little over six months and corporate recruitment wasn't the same as helping a king choose a bride.

Rosanna had left Australia under a cloud, albeit not of her making, and that weighed heavily. She couldn't squash the self-doubt that had plagued her since she'd been taken in by her ex. She should have seen through Phil. So much for her vaunted skills in assessing people! It was no excuse to admit she'd been more focused on her career than their wedding. That maybe she hadn't been as much in love as she'd first thought.

Rosanna breathed deep and focused on the positive, refusing to undermine herself this way. With her professional skills and her aunt's advice and connections, she was perfectly capable of playing fairy godmother to an aspiring Cinderella.

She just hoped the royal prince wasn't some warty toad.

That was how, in the early evening, Rosanna found herself in the back of a limousine, purring along a well-made road that skirted the capital of Dhalkur.

The sun sank over distant purple hills, gilding the ancient city and turning its shadows from amber to dark ochre and violet. Fascinated, she saw a massive crenellated city wall and beyond it a skyline of spires, domes and towers.

Rosanna looked forward to telling her parents about this place when they spoke next. They still worried about her after the scandal and her move to the UK. It would be good to divert them with something so exciting.

She swallowed hard, her throat dry despite the fruit juice and water that had been supplied for her.

This was a whole new world. Not just because she found herself in a kingdom that had, until today, been only an exotic name on a map. Even the air was different, dry, warm and faintly scented with something that made her want to take her time and fill her lungs.

From the moment she'd been collected from her aunt's house, Rosanna had entered a world of ease and luxury that she'd occasionally glimpsed courtesy of her aunt's moneyed clients but to which she didn't belong.

Never had international travel been so easy. Even the formalities of passport and customs control had been finessed by the sheikh's staff and Rosanna had spent the flight in the comfort of a private luxury jet.

Not that she'd been able to relax.

She was plagued with the disquieting feeling she'd forgotten something. But it was too late to worry whether she'd packed the right clothes to visit a royal palace.

Rosanna bit back a nervous laugh. Fortunately she wasn't important enough to stay there. She'd be in a nearby hotel, which suited her perfectly.

No, what really niggled were doubts over her preparation. She didn't feel ready, despite the hours she'd spent on the plane, reading the files on prospective matches for the sheikh from Marian's copious records. She would put in a few more hours of reading once she got to her accommodation.

Plus do more detailed research on her client.

His Majesty Sheikh Salim of Dhalkur.

Her heart dipped then rose again, pattering faster. She smiled, recognising that, despite her nerves, she was thrilled to have this opportunity. To take responsibility once more for a major project, even if one outside her previous expertise. It felt good.

As for His Majesty, she'd followed Marian's advice and concentrated so far on potential brides rather than him. Apparently the sheikh would provide information on his specific likes and dislikes after she arrived.

Nevertheless she'd feel better when she had more background on him than his name, age—thirty one—marital status—single but actively looking—and occupation—newly minted king.

She'd read about his programme of civic development and modernisation plus speculation that he'd need to be both visionary and determined to make change succeed in his staunchly traditional country. But there'd been nothing about him personally. No insights into him as a man.

The sheikh was the ultimate authority in Dhalkur. Did he also have a stranglehold on press reporting in the country?

A shiver tickled her spine. She'd dealt with powerful people, but never someone who ran his own country. Did he expect instant and total obedience?

Even the photo she'd found of him at his coronation was unsatisfactory. He'd been at a distance, a tall, proud figure standing before a crowd of jubilant citizens.

Rosanna reached for her phone, intending to do a thorough trawl for a royal photo, when the car turned into an enormous gateway and she caught her breath.

They passed through incredibly thick walls, complete with not one but two high-tech guard posts. Then they entered a long, sprawling garden.

Palms towered overhead and Rosanna caught the glint of ornamental pools beyond a screen of flowering shrubs as the car turned up to the most imposing entrance she'd ever seen.

Wide steps, tiled in azure blue, ascended to a lofty, ornamented arch, embellished with intricate carvings in shades of emerald and gold. A few metres beyond that was a slightly smaller arch, even more beautifully decorated in tones of turquoise and silver. Beyond that was a third, smaller archway, stunningly embellished with cobalt and gold, which housed a pair of studded metal doors, glowing bright bronze in the dying sunlight.

Rosanna gasped as a thrill ran through her, drawing her skin tight.

'It's amazing,' she whispered. 'I've never seen anything like it.'

The entrance was grand and architecturally magnificent with the arch within an arch, within an arch, drawing you inside before you even reached the doors. It was also simply beautiful.

'It is one of our treasures,' the chauffeur said, pride in his voice. 'It's said it took thirty artisans thirty years to complete the western entrance.'

'I feel privileged to see it,' she murmured, watching as one of the tall doors opened and a man in a long white robe emerged.

Rosanna realised the car had stopped. She met the driver's eyes in the rear-view mirror. 'Aren't we going to my hotel?'

She'd assumed he'd brought her here on the way to show her this special highlight.

'My instructions were to bring you to the palace.'

Of course it was the palace. She should have realised when they passed the security checks. Perhaps this man approaching from the grand entrance was going to provide details of her accommodation.

Her door opened and her driver invited her to get out. Beyond him was an older man with proud features and a slight smile who introduced himself as the palace chamberlain.

'Ms MacIain, welcome to Dhalkur. I hope you had a pleasant journey?'

'I did, thank you very much.'

Rosanna stepped forward only to see him turn and head back towards the imposing entrance.

'Excellent. Now, if you'll please come with me?'

'But I...' She moved quickly to keep pace. 'I thought I was going to my accommodation first.'

He paused, sweeping her with a quick, assessing look. 'So you are. You'll be a guest at the palace. It was thought more discreet and convenient.'

'Of course.'

Rosanna was pleased to find her voice sounded calm, as if she took visits to royal palaces in her stride. Not just a meeting to speak to the sheikh or one of his trusted staff, but a *stay* in a palace.

*It will be the experience of a lifetime.*

*And she'd never been more daunted in her life.*

She slid her damp palms down her lightweight trousers. It was one thing attending lavish social events organised by Marian's clients. But as she stepped under the portico of magnificent arches and saw that the workmanship and materials were even more lavish than she'd imagined, a flicker of fear flared alongside exhilaration.

Were they *jewels*, studded between the tiles? What sort of world had she entered?

Her steps faltered and the chamberlain turned, nodding when he saw her gaping up at entrance.

'Forgive me,' he said. 'I forget the impact Her Majesty's gate has on first viewing.'

Rosanna stared up at the thousands of exquisite tiles, finding images of flowers and birds picked out in iridescent colour. 'Her Majesty?'

'She lived several centuries ago. Story has it that the sheikh asked for her hand in marriage twice and each time she refused. It was only the third time that she agreed to marry, after he offered his heart along with his wealth and position. To celebrate he had this entrance made with three arches for each proposal, the last, and most beautiful, representing the joy of their eventual union. This was the entrance they used daily as they went out riding together.' He paused and pointed. 'He had her favourite stones, emeralds and lapis lazuli, set within the design.'

Not one or two but a king's ransom in gemstones. No wonder the place was well guarded!

'That's very…romantic.' And the last thing she'd expected in a country where, she'd thought, the sheikh had ultimate power. 'She must have been a remarkable woman to say no to a king.'

The chamberlain spread his hands and lifted his shoulders. 'As you say. But the sheikhs of Dhalkur have a reputation for strength and determination. Why would such a man want a weak wife?'

Which immediately made Rosanna think of her cache of files on prospective brides. Were any of them weak? She hadn't thought so but she'd better do more homework. And on her client. Was he also a strong man who wanted a feisty wife, or did he seek someone who'd defer to him?

The chamberlain shot a look at his watch and ushered her forward. 'I'm sorry to rush you, Ms MacIain, but you're expected. We cannot keep His Majesty waiting.'

Rosanna hurried forward into a mosaic-floored hallway as wide as her whole flat. 'His Majesty?'

'Yes. When he heard you'd landed he requested you attend him straight away.' Another look at his watch. 'But I fear it will be a short audience. He has another appointment soon.'

Rosanna nodded and waited till he'd turned away to surreptitiously smooth her hair back and straighten her jacket as she walked. She wished she'd had time to change into something fresh before meeting her client. More to the point, she wished she'd finished her preparation.

This wasn't what she'd expected but she'd cope. She was capable and experienced.

*But not, yet, as a fully fledged matchmaker.*

She pushed that thought aside.

Her head spun with a host of questions. About Dhalkuri sheikhs and the surprisingly romantic story she'd just heard. And about the man she was about to meet who worked late into the evening.

Unless his next appointment wasn't work but pleasure.

If that were the case it suggested he separated pleasure and his upcoming marriage. Maybe the current sheikh wasn't as much of a romantic as his ancestor.

Rosanna's curiosity burgeoned as they turned into yet another corridor. That stupendous entrance should have warned her that the palace was on a lavish scale. They seemed to walk kilometres before the chamberlain paused before a tall door of gleaming wood. He turned and caught her eye as if checking she was ready, then rapped once.

'Enter.'

The chamberlain pushed the door open and took a step inside before bowing. 'Ms MacIain is here, Your Majesty.'

'Thank you. That will be all.'

That deep voice pulled a thread of heat along Rosanna's spine and right down into her core. She told herself it was from excitement, not nerves. And definitely *not* from something familiar in the resonating timbre of that voice.

The chamberlain stepped back and gestured for her to enter, closing the door behind her.

Rosanna knew the barest amount about Dhalkuri etiquette but this she *had* checked. She stepped through the door with downcast eyes and sank into a curtsey, thankful for childhood ballet lessons that made the movement easy despite the fatigue that began to drag at her after her eventful day.

'You may approach.'

Rosanna rose on legs that suddenly felt wobbly. Something about that voice...

No time to worry about it now. She lifted her head as she stepped forward then slammed to an immediate halt.

Her eyes rounded and she had to snap her jaw shut as her mouth sagged. Because there, on the other side of a massive desk, sat not the Sheikh of Dhalkur but a man she knew.

A man she'd last seen six months earlier at a party in Scotland.

A man who'd charmed and seduced her into the most passionate kiss of her life. A man she'd been about to give herself to in her first ever sexual encounter with a stranger.

*Until he'd walked away and never returned.*

'You!' she croaked. 'What are *you* doing here?'

# CHAPTER TWO

SALIM WATCHED THE woman before him rise and felt the slam of recognition as a physical blow to his chest.

Heat ignited in his groin.

Those eyes. That mouth. The way she stood. Even the husky quality of her voice dragged him instantly back to that memorable night half a year ago.

So much had happened in six months yet he recognised her instantly. Despite her changed appearance.

Once more she wore trousers and a jacket, but there the similarity ended. There was no soft cloud of hair caressing her shoulders. No metallic silvery top catching the light like liquid mercury and drawing attention to the sweet curve of her breasts. No spike heels to complement her look of elegance melded with pure sexy siren.

She appeared all business in light grey trousers and jacket, unremarkable mid-heeled shoes and dark hair yanked back in a bun. The only hint of softness was the dark russet colour of her high-necked blouse, vivid against the dull grey.

And that moment of recognition when her mouth had softened and her eyes ate him up.

Salim's body went rigid, every muscle tensing at the sight of her and the remarkable coincidence that brought her here.

*Was* it a coincidence?

For a second he pondered the possibility she'd inveigled her way here under false pretences, then dismissed it. She'd never have got past his eagle-eyed staff.

'Good evening, Ms MacIain.' He took his time over her name, letting his tongue linger over the syllables as he watched her reaction.

There. He'd been right. Behind the shock, a blast of heat in those bright pewter eyes.

Intriguing how much he liked having that effect on her. Perhaps because his reaction to her that first night had been unprecedented. He'd attended Alistair's party to finalise a commercial deal. Not to be seduced by a temptress with silvery eyes and an allure he felt like a runnel of molten metal pouring through his veins.

Salim sat back and gestured her forward. 'You intrigue me. Who were you expecting to find in the sheikh's private study, if not me?'

She stepped closer, not with the easy poise he recalled from the party, nor the grace of her curtsey, but with short, staccato steps as if she didn't trust her balance.

'You're the Sheikh of Dhalkur? Really?'

Salim frowned. She had to ask? It didn't say much for her professionalism.

'You *are* Ms Rosanna MacIain, representing Ms Marian Best of London?'

He'd had his doubts about this project since it was mooted by his advisors. But in the circumstances it seemed the easiest way of dealing with at least one pressing obligation, giving him time to concentrate on the others.

'Yes. Yes, I am.' She stopped before his desk and

straightened her shoulders, her hands disappearing behind her back as she stood to attention.

'Then I'd expect you to know who your client is.' Salim shoved his chair back and rose. 'Is this a joke?'

Hiring a matchmaker was incredibly old-fashioned, even for Dhalkur. How did he know she hadn't come here under false pretences? He'd had experience of women finding innovative ways to invade his personal space.

Yet from the horrified look on her face, that wasn't likely. Besides, Alastair had given the company a glowing reference and so had the staff who had checked its suitability.

The firm was renowned for its phenomenal success rate and discretion. If word spread that he was actively seeking a wife, half of Dhalkur's aristocratic families would push forward their daughters and the other half would argue their merits—a sure recipe for dissension.

'I apologise… Your Majesty.'

Salim felt that breathy catch in her voice as she said his title. It was like the brush of phantom fingertips across bare skin. Like the glide of her fingers tracing his cheek and jaw, then sliding down his neck to the place where his throat tightened. He frowned, surprised to find his imagination so wayward, his response to *her* so strong.

'It's entirely my fault,' she said, shuffling her feet wider and lifting her chin. 'The circumstances that prevented Ms Best coming in person meant I was briefed at the very last moment. I spent the flight reviewing potential candidates and not—'

'Researching your employer.'

She inclined her head.

Salim frowned. 'It's not an auspicious start.' He

raised a hand when she opened her mouth to interrupt. 'I expect the best service. Discreet. Professional. Exceptional.'

'And you'll have it. Believe me, Your Majesty, we are committed one hundred percent to meeting your requirements, whatever you desire.'

A tingle of static sparked at his nape and raced down his backbone.

*Whatever you desire.*

It reminded him forcefully of what he'd desired the night they met. A desire that was unsatisfied because of the urgent news that had come out of Dhalkur, making an immediate return home necessary.

Why had Rosanna MacIain chosen that particular word?

Was it a Freudian slip? Proof that she too still felt the attraction between them?

But a king didn't dally with the hired help.

He could imagine his stern father rolling over in his grave at the thought. Those old-fashioned elders who bayed at Salim to take a bride and secure the succession would be horrified. Not at their sheikh feeling lust. But at him prioritising a foreign mistress over finding a suitable queen as soon as possible.

Salim reined in his racing thoughts.

'So you say, but your expertise remains to be proven.'

She swallowed, the movement drawing attention to the slenderness of her neck and the determined cast of her jaw.

If anyone could deliver what she promised, he had a feeling it was Rosanna MacIain, despite her lack of preparation.

It was a pity circumstances meant she'd never deliver on the unspoken promise she'd given him six months earlier. For unbridled passion. For her soft, eager body and, he was sure, pure bliss. Because their business was more important than satisfying lust. Even a lust that burned so fiercely.

He unclasped his hands and placed them palm down on the desk, annoyed more with his wandering thoughts than with her unpreparedness. After all, he'd been the one to insist she come here *immediately*.

To give himself no time to change his mind?

Being railroaded into a marriage he didn't want nettled him.

But Salim would accept the push for him to marry and provide an heir. His country needed stability.

As absolute ruler he made his own decisions but he knew the importance of following tradition where he could. Showing respect for some of the old ways would make his reform program easier, especially among traditionalists.

His elder brother, Fuad, had done untold damage with his erratic ways while their father was dying and Salim was abroad. The Royal Council had made Salim sheikh instead of Fuad because of Salim's reputation for hard work and integrity. But some were still wary. He'd spent the last few years overseas, pursuing investment opportunities and diplomatic goals for Dhalkur. Some even looked for signs that he, like Fuad, might develop signs of instability.

Which is why he would conform to expectation and take a bride.

Not just any bride. She had to be the *perfect* bride with no hint of scandal or poor behaviour in her past. Dhalkur had had enough of that with Fuad and wouldn't tolerate any more. He wanted a woman who'd be acceptable to the conservative elements who feared change, yet a woman who'd help him implement his reforms, charming foreign investors and winning the hearts of his people. Above all, a woman with whom he could spend his life.

'I have yet to sign the contract to employ you. In the circumstances I'll need to consider that carefully.'

Surprisingly, instead of bursting into hurried reassurances, Rosanna MacIain stood calmly, returning his stare confidently.

Salim's life had changed immeasurably. Returning home to his father's death, he'd been acclaimed as sheikh and lost his brother the same day. Livid at being passed over for the crown, Fuad had taken out his anger with furious speed in his favourite sports car and paid with his life.

Within a couple of days Salim had lost his family and become absolute ruler. All eyes were on him, always, seeking answers to everything his country needed. His occasional days as an almost private citizen were over.

Now few people met his gaze. Most bowed their heads in deference, whether he wanted it or not.

Maybe that's why this woman's direct stare felt unusual. Her expression was serious, as befitted doing business with a monarch. Yet Salim felt the scratch of something else beneath the surface.

Challenge?

It was an intriguing thought.

'Of course, Your Majesty. Finding a life partner is a major undertaking. When that partner will also become queen, it's even more important to choose well. Take all the time you need to consider engaging us. Naturally I'm happy to provide any further information you need about our work.'

Salim's eyebrows rose. She made it sound as if

she were graciously granting him time to dither over his decision.

Or was that sour grapes because she hadn't recognised him instantly?

It wasn't as if he preferred the idea that Rosanna MacIain had schemed her way here to pursue what they'd begun in Scotland.

He wasn't interested in an affair. Not with his work commitments.

And yet… His gaze drifted from her eyes to her mouth and that molten sensation in his belly flared hotter.

'May I ask…?'

'Yes?' He was intrigued to know what made her look suddenly uncertain, her gaze dipping to his collar.

'When you contacted Marian, Ms Best, did you know I worked with her?'

Salim took a moment to digest that. He'd never had to work hard to attract a woman who interested him. He tried to imagine concocting such an elaborate plot when instead it was women who schemed to be near him.

His brother had enjoyed manipulating people. Salim preferred to be direct. If he wanted a woman he'd tell her, not lie about needing her expertise, or use his power to his advantage.

His nostrils flared in distaste. 'You think this is a hoax? That there's no job and I contacted Ms Best as an excuse to see you again?'

She flinched and colour streaked her cheekbones. Salim was intrigued to feel his ribs tighten around his lungs as their gazes meshed.

'No, I… No. But it's an amazing coincidence that we should meet again this way.'

She was right. But he couldn't let her believe he'd

engineered this meeting to pursue an affair. The last thing he needed was a woman haunting his every move, getting in the way while he had so many important matters to juggle.

'Let me assure you that I had no idea the woman I met at Alistair's party was linked to Ms Best. Did you even work for her at the time?'

She nodded. 'I was just starting. Marian was supposed to be at the party but was held up in the States so I went in her stead.'

Now it began to make sense. 'As a representative of the company that brought Alistair and Leonie together.'

It had been Alistair's mention of the successful and utterly discreet matchmaking service which had prompted Salim to try the company himself.

Rosanna MacIain opened her mouth then paused. 'I couldn't possibly say. Marian simply asked me to attend to wish the happy couple well, and to make the acquaintance of some of the guests.' Her eyes widened and she hurried on. 'But not you. Neither of us knew you'd be there.'

Salim nodded. His visit to Scotland had been brief and low-key, out of the public eye. He'd been finalising some crucial and sensitive business deals in Europe and North America before flying home to Dhalkur.

He eyed the woman before him, admiring the way she hadn't taken the easy option to admit Alistair had been one of her company's clients, though he knew it to be so. Such reticence spoke of true discretion, the one absolute Salim insisted on in this whole archaic process.

'You're saying you had no idea who I was when we met in Scotland?' he murmured.

Salim worked to keep his private life out of the limelight but he wasn't naïve enough to believe women weren't interested in his royal status. Even when he'd been a mere prince, there was a definite cachet attached to the title. Not to mention wealth and power.

He watched something ripple across her features. What was it this contained, oh-so-professional woman fought to hide?

'Absolutely not.'

Her tone indicated that if she'd known she wouldn't have come near him. Why did that rankle?

'You're in the habit of giving yourself to a total stranger, Ms MacIain?'

Even as he said it he berated himself for stirring trouble. But there was something about her cool dismissal that he didn't like. As if what they'd shared had been easily forgotten.

*He* hadn't forgotten. Possibly because in the last six months there'd been no time to relax with a woman. His life revolved around an overfilled schedule of royal duty. That had to be the reason why the memory of their brief interlude seemed so fresh and appealing.

'I didn't *give* myself to you!'

'It felt like it.' His gaze shifted to the tight set of her mouth, remembering her fiery, luscious kisses. 'You didn't hold anything back. If we hadn't been interrupted—'

'Your recollection of the evening is rather different to mine.' Her gaze pierced him and he was reminded of the acres of burnished steel weapons in the armoury downstairs, swords, knives and lances all honed to lethal sharpness. 'I remember it being fun and—' she shrugged '—pleasant.'

'Pleasant.' Salim tested the word on his tongue and found it wanting. He shook his head. 'You underestimate yourself, Ms MacIain.'

That brought a rush of bright heat to her throat and a flare of something in her expression that might have been arousal. Or temper.

Either way, Salim discovered he liked it a lot better than her crisply businesslike attitude.

What was it about this woman that made him want to tip her off balance? He'd never been one to tease a woman, except to heighten her pleasure while making love.

He drew himself up, disturbed by the direction of his thoughts.

'Someone at that party, someone I trust, recommended your company. As I now find myself in want of a wife, I approached Ms Best. I had no idea of your connection to her.'

*In want of a wife.*

He *didn't* want a wife at all. He needed one to allay the fears of his people. Anxiety had risen when Fuad had taken control of the country during their father's terminal illness, nearly bringing the nation to ruin.

Two generations previously, the country had teetered on the brink of instability when the then sheikh had no male heir and the country faced the prospect of noble families vying to rule. His solution had been to marry his best friend's widow and adopt her son, Salim's father, as his own.

Salim's father had been a powerful and benevolent ruler, if wary of embracing change.

Dhalkur was a country which prized strong, stable government, and the government was, in effect, its sheikh. Salim would do his duty and marry, hoping to provide heirs and the promise of stability as soon as possible, while he got on with saving the country from the effects of his brother's depredations.

Salim looked at his watch. It was time for his video conference with the American investment consortium.

'We'll meet tomorrow, Ms MacIain, and I'll give you my decision.'

Her lips parted, as if to offer some persuasive argument, but instead she moistened her lips with the tip of her tongue and nodded. 'Thank you, Your Majesty.'

Salim dragged his attention away from her glistening lips, telling himself he couldn't seriously be intrigued by such an obvious ploy, if ploy it was. But now, as he surveyed her, he noted the hint of tiredness in her eyes and the strain around her mouth. If there was any ploy here it was simply the attempt of an exhausted woman to appear on top of an unexpected, taxing situation.

He pressed a buzzer on his desk and instantly the door opened, a footman appearing. 'You'll be escorted to your room. I hope you sleep well.'

'Thank you, Your Majesty.'

Then, with another deep curtsey, she was gone.

Yet it took Salim a long time, too long a time, to turn his mind to mining leases and investment options.

And long into the night he found himself wondering how well Rosanna MacIain slept in her bed under his roof.

# CHAPTER THREE

ROSANNA WAS GRATEFUL that her next meeting with
Sheikh Salim of Dhalkur wasn't scheduled until late
the next morning. It gave her time to gather her scattered wits.

The shock of finding her client was her almost-lover
from months ago had kept her awake long into the night.
In an effort to relax she'd ended up taking a long soak
in the sunken marble tub, using one of the scented bath
oils provided. But the warm water and delicate hyacinth
fragrance hadn't worked.

When she'd finally slept it had been a restless, fit-
ful slumber. She'd spent the night rolling from side to
side in a tangle of dreams that she preferred not to remember.

Because for six months he hadn't just been her
almost-lover. He'd been the man she'd dreamed about
constantly.

And in her dreams they did far more than kiss.

Only pride had stopped her from questioning her
Scottish hosts that night about their disappearing guest.
If he'd wanted to see her again he would have given her
his number and name.

Yet that night Rosanna MacIain, cautious, measured,

sensible Rosanna, had been swept up in something so glorious, so visceral, she'd forgotten everything else.

It had put what she'd once felt for Phil in perspective. Surely, if she could feel such an unstoppable need for any man, it should have been for the man she'd once planned to marry. The man who'd so deceived her.

Rosanna shuddered and tightened her grip on her laptop as she followed the footman down a long, marble-floored corridor.

Part of her discomfort was from these opulent surroundings. Everything about it reinforced the difference between her life and the rarefied world inhabited by a royal sheikh. Everything spoke of refinement and privilege. From the antique rugs to the exquisite detailing on every item, from the silver pitcher that had contained her morning juice to the heavy, embossed stationery on her desk. Even her view, of a courtyard dripping with blowsy, richly scented roses framing decorative pools and shaded seats, took her breath away.

As they walked, they passed another beautiful courtyard garden, this one filled with citrus trees in bloom. The air was heavy with the hum of bees and redolent with the scent of orange blossom.

Which reminded her of brides.

Her heart slammed her ribs.

That was the only reason she was here. To find a bride for a sheikh.

Not to spend the night imagining herself held tight in his arms. Warmth flushed Rosanna's cheeks and she stiffened her spine.

Everything depended on him signing the contract. If he turned her away before giving her a chance, she'd never forgive herself.

Despite what he thought, Rosanna *was* professional.

More to the point, she had to make this work for Marian, who'd supported her since she'd arrived in England, heartsore and distressed. Marian was relying on her now and Rosanna couldn't let her down.

Even if there was still a tiny part of Rosanna that recoiled from the idea of Salim being with another woman.

How crazy was that? It was her *job* to match him with the perfect wife.

She didn't know him, not really. Didn't even have the right to call him anything other than Your Majesty.

He didn't want her. He'd made that clear.

She told herself she felt unsettled only because of the peculiar circumstances. She was still adjusting to the reality of who he was. And to the self-knowledge he had forced on her in Scotland. That there was a side to herself she hadn't known. A live-for-the-moment hedonist willing to find bliss with a total stranger.

Rosanna firmed her lips and forced her mind back to her research this morning. She'd gleaned all she could about Salim and Dhalkur.

But while there was a lot written about the country and the previous sheikh, Salim had managed for the most part to keep under the radar of the world's press. Even though he'd spent a good part of the last couple of years overseas, she found no photos of him socialising. No paparazzi shots of him partying. Just the occasional mention in financial circles of him pursuing business interests in a number of quarters.

*As if his behaviour in Scotland wasn't the norm for him either.*

Wishful thinking, she chided herself. Just because he wasn't seen flaunting a series of lovers didn't mean he was into sexual abstinence.

*He doesn't kiss like a man who's celibate.*

Rosanna frowned. She shouldn't be thinking of her client like that. Not when it made her feel hot and bothered.

The trouble was, she found it difficult to think of Salim as her client.

Even last night when he'd made it clear this wasn't some outlandish scheme to spend time with her, she'd found it hard to get beyond remembering the pair of them together. The magnificent, hard heat of his tall frame, the softness of his lips, the knowing, coaxing, breath-stealing rightness of his kiss.

The footman knocked on a door, opened it and suddenly here she was again, entering the gracious, book-lined study.

Once more Salim sat at his desk. This time he didn't wear a western suit but a long robe and head scarf that she knew was called a *keffiyah*. It was a reminder that he was a sheikh who ruled a realm that was totally foreign to her.

The man she'd thought she'd known didn't exist. He'd been an illusion.

The story of her life, twice now drawn to men who weren't at all what she'd thought.

Yet her gaze lingered on the hard, beautiful lines of his face. His olive skin seemed darker against the stark white clothes, his spare features so compelling she found it impossible not to stare.

Abruptly he looked up from the papers before him. His eyes pinioned hers and heat fizzed in her blood.

*Just like that.*

*With no more than a look.*

Despite her stern lectures not to fantasise about him

any more. Despite her determination to cut free of the madness she'd felt on that one, solitary night.

Feeling that stirring in her blood, knowing it for weakness, evoked a deep-seated anger. At herself. And at this man who, however unwittingly, still dazzled her into unwary, unwanted thoughts.

Setting her jaw, still holding his gaze, Rosanna sank into a deep curtsey.

The door closed on the footman as Rosanna MacIain caught his gaze and a frisson of awareness feathered his nape. And backbone. And belly.

Salim set his jaw as she dipped into a curtsey so low it spoke of utter obeisance. Except her bright eyes belied that, glittering and steely as they held his.

It was provocation of the purest kind and something in him—the part that wasn't a sensible, busy ruler trying to focus on the wellbeing of his people—leapt in response.

He wanted to stride around the desk and haul her to her feet and straight into his arms. Kiss her till she turned soft and melting against him as she had that first night, purring her delight at what he did to her.

But Salim was a king. He didn't indulge in scandalous behaviour.

No matter how much he wanted to. His training and his early years in Fuad's shadow had taught him self-reliance. Acting rashly was an indulgence he couldn't permit.

'You may rise, Ms MacIain, and take a seat.'

For an instant longer he met her eyes, then forced himself to look down at the petition he'd received. The text wavered and, instead of seeing words, his brain conjured an image of bright eyes.

It wouldn't do. He wasn't like his brother, easily diverted from duty. Salim was stronger than that. He had to be, for Dhalkur's sake.

He needed a bride to quell the unease of his subjects about the lack of a royal heir. But it would be madness to employ this woman if they couldn't work together.

Firming his mouth, he closed the petition and set it aside.

But when he looked up Rosanna MacIain was the picture of professionalism. She sat with her hands loosely clasped and her back straight. She met his stare with a slight smile of acknowledgement and an air of attentiveness. No challenge. No heat in those grey eyes.

Had he imagined it?

The thought sideswiped him. Had he been *looking* for, hoping for, a personal response from her?

Surely not.

Yet he remembered how his thoughts had strayed to her again and again through last night's video conference and diplomatic reception. And later, as he lay in bed.

'I've decided to employ you.' He watched her shoulders lower on a deep exhale. Relief? Naturally. Her company's fee for a successful match was hefty. 'I've signed the contract and it's been sent to your principal.'

'Thank you, Your Majesty. I'm sure you'll be pleased with our service.'

Pleased? He'd be relieved if they found someone appropriate, someone he wouldn't mind marrying, though he couldn't get enthusiastic at the prospect of tying himself to anyone for life.

Salim pushed a document across the desk. 'All that remains is for you to sign this.'

She took it, scanning the print, her brow furrowing in concentration as she caught her bottom lip with her teeth.

He felt a flicker of something deep inside but told himself it had nothing to do with the fact that she looked…cute. More likely it was satisfaction that she was concentrating on business. That soon he'd have a bride lined up and that would be one major task sorted.

'Surely all this is covered in our standard contract.' She looked up, frowning. 'Absolute discretion is vital to our business success.'

'Nevertheless, I insist. I need to be completely sure that nothing you learn while working on my behalf finds its way beyond these walls. It's not just a matter of protecting my personal privacy. You'll learn a lot, not just about me but other people within the palace, our processes and customs. I want that protected.'

He sat back, watching as she read, wondering if she'd refuse. She took her time and Salim felt respect rise. Many people in the presence of royalty were too eager to agree to whatever was proposed. He liked that this woman chose to inform herself about what she'd be agreeing to.

Salim saw her eyebrows rise. 'The penalties for disclosure are incredibly harsh.'

He shrugged. 'You're in my world now, Ms MacIain, and I value my privacy.'

She nodded. 'Very well.' Seconds later she'd pulled out a pen, placed the document on the desk and signed it. 'There you are.'

He reached out and drew the agreement to him, noting her neat signature. Strange the sense of deep satisfaction he felt. Almost as if she'd signed away something other than her guarantee of discretion.

Shaking off the odd sensation, he nodded. 'Excellent. Now we can begin. What do you want to proceed?'

'First it's important to know what you're looking for in a wife. Your likes and dislikes. Any dealbreakers, things that mean you wouldn't consider a particular woman no matter what else she brings to the table.'

'Such as?'

'That's up to you.' When he didn't add anything she continued. 'For instance, some men prefer a woman who hasn't publicly been in a committed relationship.'

'You mean, they want a virgin?'

She shrugged.

He watched the hint of colour appear in her cheeks as she met his gaze, though her narrowed stare looked disapproving. Did she think him one of those? Perhaps she thought his country so traditional that no one other than a virgin would be considered.

Either way, Salim felt a niggle of distaste at the assumption. She hadn't called him hidebound, she was too adroit for that. But otherwise, why raise it?

Then he swallowed a huff of wry amusement at the idea of setting Ms MacIain to ask potential wives if they were virgins. It would serve her right if he did.

'We'll leave the issue of sexual experience aside for now. What else?'

After a pause she began to reel off a list. Did he have a time frame? Advisors to help him make his decision? Would he travel or meet women in Dhalkur? Would he meet them together or separately?

'You plan to parade them before me?' He'd thought himself prepared for this process. Now he wasn't sure.

'Certainly not. This isn't a beauty pageant,' she snapped, and Salim felt a flicker of relief.

'Good. I want to get to know them, spend time with them, before I make any decisions.'

How he'd find time to do that with his current schedule remained to be seen. But this was important so he'd find a way. He had no intention of saddling himself with a woman who was a total stranger.

'Once I have your answers to those, and a few other questions, I can proceed. I'll need a contact in your office to ensure anything I arrange fits with your schedule.'

'Taqi, my assistant, will meet you to discuss options. He'll be the one making arrangements, not you.'

'But I—'

'That's not negotiable, Ms MacIain. You can pursue your contacts but arrangements to meet these women will be made via my office.' When she made to respond, Salim raised his hand. 'Unless you fancy yourself an expert on royal protocol as well as matchmaking?'

Again that spark in her gaze, turning dark grey irises to startling silver. Salim had always thought grey a cool colour but he now associated it with fire and restrained temper. Fascinating.

It would be petty to enjoy having the last word. Instead he moved to business.

'The time frame is as soon as possible. You'll report directly to me. No one else will be involved.' He imagined marrying a woman chosen by committee and shuddered. 'I don't want this to become a matter of speculation in Dhalkur.'

*Especially if the search failed.*

'I won't travel beyond my borders for the next few months though I'm not averse in principle to seeing someone in their own environment.'

'I see.' She surveyed him carefully. 'That will make the task more difficult.'

'Just tell me if you're not up to it, Ms MacIain.'

There it was again, that flash of temper, quickly hidden. Salim shouldn't enjoy provoking it, yet he preferred it to that coolly assessing stare of hers, as if her only interest in him was as a business client.

*That's all you are now, remember?*

*You walked away from her the night you got the news your father was dying. Whatever you thought you shared is long over.*

It didn't feel over. It felt real, that simmering stew of desire in his groin, that hyper-awareness.

Salim drew a deep breath, steepling his hands under his chin, forcing his thoughts back to the task in hand.

'You mistake me—'

'Then you *do* feel up to managing this task? Good. As for it being difficult, yes, I agree. That's why I was persuaded to hire in your particular expertise.'

He paused to let her digest that.

'There are ways we can bring the candidates to Dhalkur without gossip or unnecessarily raised expectations. There will be a festival here in the capital soon. Traditionally it's a celebration for the Dhalkuri people but this year we're expanding it to showcase business, investment and research opportunities to the wider world.'

It was a new direction for Dhalkur and there were still sceptics but Salim was determined to make it work.

'In association with that we're hosting a range of cultural, scientific and leisure events that we hope will attract foreign interest.'

He watched her expression change. Her pursed

mouth softened into a slow smile and her eyes lit, not with impatience but approval.

Salim told himself it was interesting to observe the turnaround in her. It wasn't that he liked the quick way she grasped the potential opportunities, or the fact he could easily read her changing mood.

No, this wasn't personal. It was simply important they were on the same wavelength.

'So,' she mused, 'there will be a range of events that might bring all sorts of women to Dhalkur.'

Salim inclined his head. 'Either by specific invitation, or at the suggestion of business or cultural contacts.'

'Which your assistant can arrange?'

Salim smiled. 'He's a man with many contacts.'

She sat back in her seat, nodding, her eyes fixed on a distant point as if visualising something he couldn't see. 'I like your thinking. Lots of people. Lots of events. A chance to socialise and even, perhaps, see some of the women working among their peers.'

Salim's mouth hooked up in wry amusement. In six months no one had treated him like this, as an equal rather than a ruler. No one except his cousin, Tara, now queen of the neighbouring country of Nahrat.

What would Tara make of Rosanna MacIain? He had an inkling the pair had a lot in common, both straight-talking, neither easily intimidated, even by a king. In Tara's case her determination had led her to escape the clutches of his appalling brother but then put her in conflict with the powerful Sheikh of Nahrat, whom she'd eventually fallen in love with and married.

Maybe after all, she and Ms MacIain didn't have so much in common.

'I'm glad to win your approval, Ms MacIain.'

That made her start and turn her focus on him.

Did he imagine a fizz of warmth beneath his skin in response to that bright stare?

'It's a great idea. But if this festival starts soon there's no time to waste.' She began making notes. 'Let's start with what sort of woman you want. We need to narrow the options.'

Salim didn't have a coy bone in his body but it felt plain *wrong* to have this woman questioning him on that particular topic.

Because the woman who came instantly to mind when he thought of attraction was *her*.

'What about physical preferences?'

'I don't have a favourite type. Some women are just more appealing than others. It's not necessarily a matter of appearance.'

Often it was as much about personality. An intellectual equal, not afraid to voice an opinion. Or a great sense of humour, that appealed too.

She looked unconvinced. 'I'm sorry if this feels too intimate. Especially as we're strangers.'

She paused and Salim silently corrected her. That was the problem, he realised. They *weren't* strangers. They *had* been intimate. He remembered the feel of her body against his, her taste—

'But we need to specify these things.' Her lips turned up in a brief smile. 'Surely it's better to be a little uncomfortable now than waste your time later if I introduce you to women who just don't light a spark with you?'

Inevitably Salim's thoughts veered to that night in Scotland. To the sparks he'd felt as they flirted. Then the conflagration of desire as they melded in each other's arms. Even leaving the estate, his thoughts turning to

Dhalkur and his ailing father, he'd watched fireworks explode against the dark sky and known that if he'd stayed with his fascinating, sultry stranger, he'd be experiencing another sort of fireworks in her bed.

His fascinating, sultry stranger now looked as if she bit back annoyance. Who could blame her? She'd been hired to introduce him to suitable women and he couldn't even articulate a definition of suitable.

'Blonde,' he blurted out. 'I like blondes.'

His last lover had been blonde.

Rosanna's eyebrows rose. 'Anything else?'

She looked like a long-suffering teacher, barely restraining impatience with a slow pupil.

'Some height. I don't want a permanent kink in my neck from bending down to kiss her.'

Though at the moment, he seriously doubted this scheme would produce a woman he'd want to kiss at every opportunity. This would be a marriage of convenience. He didn't expect romance, or set-the-world-alight passion. Yet Rosanna was right, for his own sake he needed to find someone he could live with, permanently. He wanted mutual respect, affection and, yes, attraction.

She raised her eyebrows. 'That's it? Blonde and not short? It's not much to work with.'

Salim bit back the urge to tell her the truth. That at the moment what he wanted was a woman with dark, cloud-soft hair and eyes that glittered first dark pewter then silver as her mood changed. A woman whose kisses were fiery and demanding, but who felt almost vulnerable in his arms.

Arms that ached, not, he assured himself, with emptiness, but with tension at being put through this undignified trial.

'I'm not used to choosing women like they're items on a menu.'

That startled her. Salim watched her eyes darken and her mouth soften as if he'd surprised and pleased her. Was that understanding he read on her face?

For a moment he felt again the sense of communion that he'd experienced in Scotland. It eased the edginess in his belly.

'Fair enough. Are you sure there are no negatives you want to specify?'

'A high-pitched giggle,' he found himself saying. 'It grates. I once spent an evening at an official dinner next to a woman who kept tittering at me.'

He'd ended up with a sore jaw from grinding his teeth.

'Maybe she was nervous. You can be rather daunting.' At his stare she hurried on. 'Being royal and so on.'

Except he'd been incognito and the girlish giggle had been an unsuccessful attempt to appear cute and helpless. Personally he preferred a woman who didn't feel the need for a protector. He liked a woman with spirit.

Rosanna sat straighter, rolling her shoulders as if they'd grown tight. 'Okay, Your Majesty. Can you tell me anything you *do* want, if you can't specify physical attributes?'

'Ideally?' Salim muffled a laugh. 'The aim is to find someone acceptable to me and suitable as my queen. That's a long list.'

Anticipation sparkled in her eyes. 'Try me.'

He shrugged. 'She must be someone who won't be overwhelmed by life as a royal. Someone either born to such a position or who already lives a high-profile life. She must cope with the stresses of life at court and being in the public eye.'

Rosanna's eyes narrowed. 'So she must be royal or aristocratic.'

Her tone gave nothing away but Salim suspected she thought him elitist. He felt a tiny burr of discomfort under his skin.

'Yes. Or from a humble background, as long as she's now used to moving in privileged circles. Not someone who's going to be overawed by the pomp and ceremony of life as my queen.'

He didn't care about her pedigree, but he didn't have time to hold his wife's hand if she felt overwhelmed. This would be no love match. He didn't believe in love, not for himself. He *needed* someone who could adapt effortlessly and hit the ground running.

'Not someone self-absorbed,' he continued. 'I need someone who thinks about what others want and need.'

Did he imagine her mouth pinched at the corners as she typed? 'Someone attentive to your needs then.'

'I'm not looking for a servant, Ms MacIain.' Her head jerked up as if pulled on a string and he saw that's precisely what she'd thought. 'I have a palace full of people to cater to my needs. I was thinking of someone interested in my people's needs.'

'Of course. I understand.'

Rosanna ducked her head again, making another note, but not before Salim caught a flush of colour on her cheeks.

'But yes, since you mention it,' he relented. 'Someone interested and willing to listen to my needs, as I hope to take an interest in hers. I want a partner, Ms MacIain, as far as that's possible.'

Salim hadn't thought about it in those terms before, but that was exactly what he needed. He'd spent his life training to serve his country but he was no fool. Things would be easier with someone to share his burdens.

Burdens that were so much heavier thanks to his brother's instability and excesses. Instead of inheriting a stable kingdom, Salim had to deal with a level of fear and volatility that were legacies of Fuad's period in control.

Yet Salim wasn't searching for a soul mate. He didn't believe in them.

Life had made him a loner. The early death of his mother. A decent but distant father, preoccupied with governing. A spiteful elder brother who'd resented him and found endless opportunities to torment and torture him. Salim had survived by drawing in on himself, becoming self-reliant, guarding himself by expelling obvious signs of weakness that could be exploited.

That meant he never opened up his deepest self to others. Survival had meant maintaining a level of reserve even with friends.

'I want someone attractive, interesting, willing to listen but also to contribute to conversation as a hostess. By that I don't just mean wearing fancy clothes and attending royal events. But someone who can put people at ease when, as you say, they might be daunted by royalty.'

Salim fixed Rosanna with a stare. Her earlier reference to him being daunting had been a thinly veiled personal jab.

'Someone who can hold their own and keep an even temper in difficult social situations. But not a pushover. She must be strong enough to demand respect and receive it graciously.'

He paused, listening to the light click of computer keys. Really, there was too much to list.

'I need a woman with an unblemished background. It's absolutely vital she has no past scandals or gossip dogging her.'

Did he imagine that Rosanna stiffened? Surely that went almost without saying.

'Someone who likes people. Who is patient with strangers wanting to see her or tell her their stories, even if she's tired. There will be times, when we are touring the provinces, in particular, when the days will be long and the demands of the public high. I need someone who can be gracious and caring.'

'She must speak your language, then?'

'Ideally yes, or able to learn it.'

He watched her add a note. 'Someone from this region then, or with linguistic skills to help her fit in.'

Salim shrugged. 'That would be easiest, but if they fit the other criteria, I'm happy as long as they're willing to learn and respect our ways.'

He wasn't hung up on nationality. In fact, he'd always had more affinity with women he'd met outside his country, perhaps because they weren't so obsessed with his royal position.

Personally he wanted a woman who wasn't afraid to express herself, including when it came to seeking pleasure. But there were more important criteria to be satisfied first.

He looked up to find Rosanna waiting for a response. 'Sorry?'

'I asked if there was anything else. It's quite a long list for someone initially unwilling to give specifics.'

Salim felt his mouth tug up in a smile. That was exactly what he meant. No Dhalkuri woman would talk to him like that. Rosanna MacIain made a refreshing change.

Not, of course, that she was on his list of potential brides.

'In the interests of making sure you earn your salary, let me add a few more. Kindness.' He ticked off his thumb. 'I'd like to marry someone with a good heart. Reasonable intelligence and education.' He ticked a second finger. 'I don't want someone who will flounder trying to understand the political, diplomatic and social issues around them.'

'A very well-rounded woman, then,' she said under her breath.

Did he detect a sour note? No matter. She'd asked what he needed and he was obliging. He raised a third finger.

'Stylish, or with potential to be so with some assistance. As my queen she will be in the spotlight a lot. So, confident too.' He raised a fourth finger. 'A wilting violet won't do at all.'

'Anything else, Your Majesty?'

Yes, there was a definite crispness in her voice. Strange how much he enjoyed hearing it.

Everything he said was completely true. But he rather enjoyed setting the bar high and seeing her reaction. Would she rise to the challenge?

'Now you mention it, yes. The most important of all.'

She looked up from her typing and, as her gaze met his, Salim felt a tightening deep in his body that took him straight back to Scotland and her total abandon in his arms. It made his next words emerge with a gravel edge.

'She must be willing and able to have children.'

# CHAPTER FOUR

*WILLING AND ABLE to have children.*

His words echoed in Rosanna's ears for the hundredth time, making her insides roll over.

It wasn't the memory of the gruff ultra-masculine timbre of his voice that made the fine hairs at her nape rise. Of course not. It was the sheer sense of arrogant entitlement embodied in his requirement. Willing and able to have children.

Would he insist on a medical examination?

It seemed outlandish and outdated. Yet, now she'd been here a couple of days and learned about the importance of the monarchy in Dhalkur, she understood the sheikh's desire to have heirs soon.

Male heirs, of course.

What if his poor spouse only provided females?

On the upside, Rosanna suspected that his wife would find a good deal of enjoyment trying for those heirs. She could attest that Sheikh Salim of Dhalkur was a man who knew women and how to please them. His bride would probably consider intimacy with him one of the major pluses of marriage.

Rosanna flattened her lips, ignoring the shimmy of female reaction deep inside. It wasn't her concern.

Her concern was arranging for His Majesty to meet the woman of his dreams.

If that were possible!

Any woman who actually met all his requirements would be a paragon. Rosanna seriously doubted she'd find anyone who could meet every item on his wish list. For a man who initially demurred at stating his qualifications for a bride, he'd sure warmed to the task.

Her already difficult job seemed to grow tougher by the day. Especially as, after two days, Salim hadn't been available for a follow-up meeting. Yet, until he gave approval, she wouldn't make arrangements to invite any of the women she had in mind to Dhalkur.

'His Majesty will see you now, Rosanna.'

She looked up to see the sheikh's personal assistant in the doorway. Instantly she got to her feet. 'Wonderful. Thanks, Taqi.'

He'd been an enormous help, clarifying details about the upcoming festival, Dhalkuri customs and royal protocol. As a result, Rosanna had been able not only to put together a list of potential brides, but a plan that would allow Salim to meet them without it being obvious he was looking for a wife.

Taqi inclined his head gravely and something about his assessing expression made her pause.

Did he finally recognise her as the woman his boss had been kissing that night in Scotland?

She'd recognised him because Salim had called him by name that night and it had stuck in her mind. Now she wondered if, despite the darkness and Salim's attempt to shelter her with his body, his assistant knew about those moments of madness.

Heat flushed her throat.

'Is everything okay?' she asked.

'Yes, of course. It's just…' He shook his head. 'It's been a busy few days for His Majesty. Try to keep it short.'

Reluctantly Rosanna nodded. There was a lot to discuss and she'd hoped to get sign-off on it all tonight. But she was aware Taqi had squeezed her in after the sheikh's final official event.

'I'll do my best.'

He nodded, his face breaking into an approving smile. She realised he wasn't just an efficient assistant. He genuinely cared about the sheikh's wellbeing. Nor was he the only one. The other people she'd dealt with in the last two days admired and respected their sovereign.

As she followed Taqi down an unfamiliar corridor, she realised it made her feel good, knowing others approved of Salim. That had been her first reaction too. Not just that dazzle of sexual attraction, but *liking*. She'd enjoyed their banter, his insightful comments, wry humour and easy charm.

After he left she'd decided she must have been wrong about him. Just as she'd been wrong about Phil. Familiar doubts had surfaced about her flawed judgement in both cases, eating away at the fragile self-confidence she'd worked hard to rebuild since leaving Sydney for the UK.

That was one good thing to come out of this bizarre situation. Learning Salim's identity and realising his sudden departure in Scotland was linked to his father's death. He must have been called back that night to a deathbed. Her indignation and hurt at being so easily brushed aside vanished in face of that knowledge.

Taqi knocked on a door, opened it and gestured for her to enter.

Thanking him, Rosanna stepped through, then

stopped, eyes widening as the door clicked closed behind her.

She'd expected an office. Instead it was a lounge room. Large by normal standards, it felt pleasingly intimate with a grouping of comfortable-looking sofas, glowing lamps, a scatter of papers across a side table and plates of food on a low table at the centre of the sofas.

But what made her chest contract was Salim. He wore black, tailored trousers and a formal shirt undone just enough to reveal a tantalising V of dark golden flesh. A silk bow tie dangled loose at the collar and his dark hair was rumpled as if he'd run his hands through it.

Or as if some woman had.

Rosanna's gaze skimmed the room but there was no one else here. A door on the other side of the room caught her attention. Did it lead to a bedroom? Had his lover slipped through there?

Why that mattered, she refused to consider.

He looked up and she saw he was chewing. Golden lamplight highlighted the movement of his strong throat and Rosanna felt a strange trembling inside.

She'd had two days to push her unresolved feelings for this man into a locked box. She'd done it well enough during the day. It was only her dreams she hadn't been able to control. But now, entering what looked like his personal domain late in the evening, discovering that he looked every bit as delectable as he had that night six months ago, jarred her confidence.

'Your Majesty.'

The words sounded strident, too abrupt, and Rosanna hid a wince as she sank into a curtsey.

'Please, Ms MacIain—' he rose and gestured for

her to take the sofa side-on to his '—have a seat.' He smiled and her body responded as a galloping heat raced through her. 'I hope you'll excuse me snacking as we talk. I missed my evening meal when a crisis cropped up.'

Rosanna sank onto the lounge. Shame rose at her earlier suspicion that he'd avoided her because he hadn't relished their earlier discussion, addressing personal issues. And at her imagining him busy with a lover.

Now she looked beyond his flagrant sex appeal and she noticed lines of weariness around his mouth and a hint of shadows beneath his eyes.

'It must be tough, taking on responsibility for a whole country,' she blurted, then snapped her mouth closed, horrified at how her thoughts had slipped out.

Salim's eyes widened and he paused with a piece of flatbread in his hand. Belatedly she wondered if anyone was ever so frank with him. She was sure the answer was *no*.

Then his shoulders lifted in the tiniest of shrugs. 'It has its moments. This has been a particularly demanding week.'

'I'm sorry… I—'

'Don't apologise. It's refreshing to have someone say what's on their mind. Most people are cautious expressing themselves around royalty.'

Rosanna winced. Usually she was more circumspect. What was it about this man that made her respond without thinking? She was struggling to convince him she could do this job. She didn't need to plant more seeds of doubt in his head. 'Nevertheless, Your Majesty, it's none of my business and—'

'Please. It's late and it's been a long day. Shall we

dispense with the formality, Rosanna?' He paused. 'If you don't mind me calling you Rosanna?'

*Mind?* How could she mind when the sound of her name in that dark, velvety voice sent a wash of eagerness through her? When the way he spoke her name made her sound like a glamorous, seductive stranger, not the ordinary woman she was. She felt her skin tighten and something deep within her clench.

She *should* mind. She should do everything she could to keep distance between them. Not that she feared him, more that she didn't trust her reactions to him.

'If you prefer, Your Majesty.'

She looked down at the laptop on the cushion beside her and pulled it close, determined to focus on business.

'I *do* prefer.' Rosanna felt his gaze touch her face but didn't look up, pretending to be busy with her computer. 'When we're alone, you needn't bother to curtsey and I prefer that you call me Salim.'

That jerked her head up. She met eyes the colour of a midnight sky. Rosanna had the disturbing sensation that if she looked long enough she'd fall into those inky depths and not want to come back to reality.

'Your Majesty seems far too formal after what we shared.'

*And there it was, out in the open.*

*Everything she had tried to forget.*

Or if not forget, then at least pretend hadn't happened.

The air rushed from her lungs, as if in relief. Yet her pulse hammered too fast. Surely the only way they could work together was if they forgot what had passed between them in Scotland? Surely mentioning that kiss, and the embrace that was far more than a kiss, opened a Pandora's box that was better left closed?

Because, while it might have meant little to him, Rosanna struggled not to be distracted by the memory of passion more urgent than she'd ever known. Even when she'd been engaged to marry the man she'd thought she loved...

She swallowed and moistened her bottom lip with her tongue. 'Do you really think it's wise to drop those barriers?'

The sheikh's eyebrows shot up and the hint of a smile on his mouth flattened.

'Don't overcomplicate things, Rosanna.' He paused on her name as if daring her to disagree. 'I'm simply aiming to make our working relationship easier. Let me assure you I don't expect anything from you except your matchmaking skills.'

*That was her told.*

Whatever had drawn them together before clearly no longer existed for him. Maybe what had seemed to Rosanna a once in a lifetime experience was for him nothing out of the ordinary. A little flirting to pass the time.

'Is that clear?'

His voice was crisp, so different to the sultry voice of seduction at their first meeting.

'Perfectly, Your Majesty.'

His eyebrows rose in an imperious slant. Clearly he'd heard the huffiness in her tone. Just as clearly he was used to instant, unquestioning obedience.

A chill raced down Rosanna's backbone. This man truly was ruler of all he surveyed, the absolute authority in his country. If she didn't satisfy him, if he judged her work to be below par, it would be her aunt as well as she who paid the price.

'I understand, Salim.'

She swallowed, ignoring the thickness in her throat and the burr of excitement at the taste of his name on her tongue. She had to end this now, stop remembering what had been and concentrate on business.

'I have a preliminary shortlist for you to consider.'

'Already? Excellent.'

Did she detect surprise? As if he hadn't expected her to produce any options so soon?

Rosanna didn't know whether to be annoyed at his apparently low expectations or pleased to surprise him.

'Do you have time to go through it now?' Rosanna remembered his assistant warning her to keep this meeting short. 'Or would you prefer to look at the material in your own time? I can email you the profiles.'

He shook his head. 'Let's get this started.'

Yet he didn't sound eager, she mused as she opened her laptop. Not like a man excited to find his perfect match.

But this was a business arrangement. Finding a bride to fulfil a set of requirements. She'd heard no sentimentality as he talked of finding a wife.

Salim wasn't seeking a love match.

Yet, a voice whispered in her mind, it wouldn't be entirely business.

She looked up as Salim plucked a bunch of grapes from a bowl and lounged back, picking one grape at a time and popping them into his mouth.

The lamplight accentuated the hard angle of his jaw as he chewed. His powerful body sprawled in an attitude of utter relaxation. His bow tie dangled like a sexy invitation against the V of enticing skin at his open collar and her fingers twitched.

He looked flagrantly male and provocatively sensual. Change the clothes and he could model for a pampered pasha in some erotic story, waiting for a concubine to please him through the night.

'Rosanna? Are you ready?'

Heat rushed up her throat and into her cheeks as glittering dark eyes snared hers. A thump of something smacked her chest and she ducked her head.

What a shame she'd pulled her hair back off her face. If it had been down it might have masked her reaction.

*Like a virgin who's never seen a sexy man.*

At least he had no way of knowing what had produced her furious blush.

'Yes, absolutely ready.' She put the laptop on the corner of the table between them, turned to face him. 'Here's our first candidate.'

Any hope she'd had that this might be easy faded as Salim rejected the first three women before she'd even finished reciting all their details.

He wasn't unreasonable, but nor was he as easygoing as his casual sprawl suggested. The man had a mind like a steel trap and an unerring eye for detail. Details that had him dismissing contenders quickly.

Rosanna busied herself, making notes on his observations and preferences. She was getting a better feel for his likes and dislikes now they were talking specifics. That would help inform her search.

'You think I'm being unduly difficult?'

She looked up to find him watching her, the intensity of his dark gaze at odds with his indolent sprawl. He reminded her of a large, predatory cat, ostensibly at rest, until you noticed his laser-sharp focus.

Rosanna had always been a sucker for an intelligent, quick-thinking man. In her experience they were competent and resourceful, both qualities she found hugely sexy.

*But not in an employer.*

*Not when she was being paid to find him a woman.*

Rosanna cleared her throat. 'Not at all. You're making an important choice and I appreciate your decisiveness.' Memories of recruitment processes where decision makers had dithered were vivid in her mind. 'This is very helpful.'

Besides, she hadn't been foolish enough to present her best candidates first. She knew enough to give him time to settle and begin to think clearly about his wants and needs.

'So, who have you next?'

Rosanna leaned forward and brought up the profile of the next candidate, one who hadn't been on her original list but who was a natural contender for Salim's queen. Her portrait filled the screen. It was an informal shot, showing a warm smile, pretty face and dark eyes sparkling with humour.

'I took a chance with this one. She's not blonde or particularly tall, but she ticks so many other boxes.'

On paper she seemed perfect. Yet Salim didn't look impressed.

'Princess Amina? You're telling me she's on your matchmaking books? She's a client of yours?'

'No. But this isn't a dating service. I'm not here to find a husband for someone on our books, though it's a possibility. My sole focus is to find you the right wife, whether it's someone previously known to us or not.'

His look of surprise made Rosanna wonder again if he had low expectations of their service. If so, why engage them?

She was determined to do the best job possible. It wasn't just her aunt's business that rode on a successful outcome. Rosanna's personal competence was on trial.

This was her first major test after the cataclysmic blow to her ego and reputation in Australia. Her confidence was shaky, and she needed this success to shore up her sense of self-worth.

Rosanna took a deep breath and looked Salim straight in the eye. He might be all-powerful and prefer to ask questions instead of answer them. But he was a client and she needed to understand his requirements and his doubts.

'Your Majesty. Salim. Am I missing something? Is there some reason you think us incapable of doing this job properly?'

The slight rise of those straight dark eyebrows told Rosanna he wasn't used to being questioned. Was he offended? Or surprised that she'd read his response?

Rosanna took a calming breath, marshalling the patience she had perfected in dealing with difficult men in the corporate world. 'If there's a problem I would rather you were frank about it so I can deal with the issue. Then we can focus on achieving the outcome you want.'

'You're right,' he said. 'I apologise. The process of hiring a matchmaking service seems outmoded. Though your company was recommended, in my mind there's still a disconnect between the idea of serious business and something as nebulous as matchmaking.'

Before she could respond, he went on. 'Plus, I'm not comfortable talking about my personal life and preferences. Blame my upbringing or my family circumstances. And, as you'll appreciate, in the past, choosing a woman has always been intensely private.'

Rosanna blinked. 'Thank you for being so frank.'

Despite her hopes she hadn't expected it.

Her mind buzzed with questions about his family circumstances which she would *not* be asking. No matter how much she wanted to know. As for him choosing a woman, she'd been on the receiving end and could vouch for the fact it was indeed very private. Despite telling herself not to, she still hoarded that particular memory to herself as if it were precious.

'I totally understand your discomfort at discussing such personal matters. Though I work in the field I'm not sure how easy I'd find it to use a matchmaking service.'

She'd always assumed she'd simply meet the right man, they'd fall in love and everything would be straightforward. That had happened, except Phil hadn't been the right man and it had been anything but straightforward.

Rosanna's flesh crawled at the memory and she forced her thoughts to Salim, watching her steadily. She liked his direct stare, she realised, even when it made her self-conscious. Better a man who looked you in the eye than…

'I assure you my questions are solely so I can get the right outcome for you.' Rosanna spread her hands. 'As for this being an outmoded industry, you'd be surprised.'

She had been, when she'd started working for her aunt.

'Matchmaking has been around for thousands of years and probably will be in the future. It offers cool logic and careful assessment. As well as introducing people who might not otherwise meet, it's a safety mechanism when so many people rush into marriage because of lust or blind hope.'

Salim sat forward. 'That sounds almost…disenchanted. Don't you believe in love? Or attraction as a starting point for a relationship?'

*Do you?* she wondered. But she already had her answer. Love wasn't on Salim's agenda.

His dark stare captured hers and Rosanna felt that familiar fire ignite in her body. It took all her discipline not to squirm in her seat and reveal her discomfort. Because even now he made her feel things, urges and wants, no other man made her feel.

'Not disenchanted.' More disappointed, but she wasn't going there. Rosanna refused to relive the fiasco of her private life with Salim. 'Just sensible and careful. Our aim is to do our best so our clients are happy in the long-term, not just in the beginning.'

He looked like he wanted to ask more. Could he sense she avoided a direct answer? But to her relief he eventually nodded and turned his attention to the screen.

'So, tell me about the princess. Why you think she's such a good match?'

Rosanna dragged in a relieved breath. Being in the spotlight of that searing scrutiny made her simultaneously nervous and thrilled. Would she ever be able to meet him and *not* react like a smitten woman?

'Princess Amina is a strong contender. She's well educated. She's from a neighbouring kingdom so knows the region and the politics, has diplomatic skills and is used to being in the public eye. She meets your requirement of looking good in public and from what I've been able to find she's kind and has a sense of humour, both pluses in a partner.'

Salim inclined his head. 'You *have* done your homework. I wouldn't have thought of her.'

Rosanna frowned. That seemed odd. Had he assumed she would only put forward western women? Could it be that was why she'd been hired? Maybe all

his years abroad had given him a preference for foreign women.

*And maybe that's wishful thinking.*

'Anything else?'

Rosanna looked at her notes, not that she needed to.
'She also seems to be in good health.'

That was as far as Rosanna would go towards specu-
lating on her ability to bear children.

'Unfortunately you've missed one major consider-
ation.'

'I have?'

She frowned. She'd spent hours not just looking up
the princess's CV but trawling for references to her
character and interests.

Salim nodded. 'Her older sister.'

Rosanna shook her head. 'Well,' she said slowly, 'you
*could* consider her. However, from what I gather she
wouldn't make an attractive spouse.' By all accounts
the elder sister was selfish, overindulged and petulant.
'I'm not sure she has the qualities you're after.'

Salim's mouth curled into a smile that was as devastating as it was sudden. It was so full of amusement that
Rosanna felt her lips twitch in response. Those ebony
eyes beckoned with humour, banishing any last trace
of formality between them.

A tiny inner voice cried out *danger*. Yet her body
listed closer, drawn by the crackling current of energy
between them.

'That's the understatement of the decade.' His eyes
danced in a way that did strange things to Rosanna's
internal organs. 'She's moody, self-important and very
pushy. She's also convinced she'd make a perfect queen
for Dhalkur, despite my views on the matter.'

Rosanna felt her eyes widen. 'She tried…?'

He shrugged, his humour fading abruptly. 'Let's not go into details. I'll just say that the idea of being closely connected to that family doesn't appeal.'

Rosanna wondered what the older princess had done. *Pushy* made it sound like she'd made an effort to ingratiate herself with Salim.

Had she set out to snare him? Maybe seduce him?

Rosanna's teeth ground at the thought. Until she realised what she was doing. Yet the feeling of outrage persisted. Why? Not out of protectiveness. Salim was a powerful man who could look out for himself.

It couldn't be…jealousy, could it? That was impossible.

Yet the ache in her jaw, the hot flush in her belly and the tension from her nape to her shoulder blades signalled something unprecedented. Something she'd never experienced before.

Horrified, she jerked back, one arm flying out in an instinctive gesture of protest, and the laptop slid off the table.

Rosanna crouched down, reaching for it, and collided with Salim, doing the same thing. Their shoulders bumped, their hands meeting on the metal surface.

Rosanna froze as his hand covered hers.

Suddenly she couldn't hear anything over the harsh sound of her breathing and the pound of her pulse. Her fingers twitched as long fingers circled her wrist.

The air caught in her lungs as she forced herself to look up. Those midnight eyes were on her, bright but enigmatic. He was so close she felt the warm waft of his breath on her cheek. Could see the tiny individual dark hairs of his night-time stubble just beginning.

Her palms itched to reach out and touch him there,

run her hand over his jaw and feel the raspy friction against her flesh.

The thought of it sent a luxurious shiver tumbling down her spine and rolling through her belly.

All the feelings she'd tried to suppress around this man burst back into roaring life. Breathless anticipation. Desire so profound she felt it as an ache in her womb and a dampness between her thighs.

She needed to break this stasis. She told herself mere seconds had elapsed, that all she had to do was move. But it felt like she was in a bubble, encased in a space where nothing existed but her and him, not even time.

Salim swallowed and Rosanna followed the movement of his throat muscles as if mesmerised. How could such a simple thing be so deeply arousing?

Desperately she moistened her lips, trying to find sensible words. Instead she heard, 'Rosanna,' in a deep, hoarse voice that drew her nipples tight.

Her rush of yearning jarred her free.

She stumbled to her feet, grabbing the lounge to pull herself up then wobbling on her heels as if her ankles were made of jelly and these weren't her most comfortable, familiar work shoes.

By the time she straightened Salim was standing, holding out her laptop. His face was unreadable as she took it, careful not to touch his hands.

'It's late.' His voice was firm and easy. She must have imagined that rough edge to it. 'Send me the profiles and I'll look at them in my own time and get back to you.'

'Of course.' She fought a cringe and instead pulled her mouth up in what she hoped looked like a smile. She nodded, her gaze on a point near his ear. 'Yes, that's good,' she gabbled. 'I'll…wait to hear from you.'

Sheer willpower helped her walk from the room, head up and back straight. All she could do was hope that Salim had no idea how close she'd come to ignoring pride and her job and the fact he wasn't interested in her.

That she'd almost thrown herself into his arms and begged him to make love to her.

# CHAPTER FIVE

'I MUST CONGRATULATE YOU, Your Majesty, on your plans for the upgraded medical facility.'

Salim met a pair of blue eyes in a smiling face. 'Thank you, Doctor. I have hopes it will make a difference to Dhalkur.'

The doctor shook her head, her golden hair slipping around her shoulders. 'Please, call me Ingrid.'

'Thank you, Ingrid.'

In her elegant, red dress and high heels she looked more like a model than a paediatric specialist. And, he was pleased to see, she'd been at ease at this evening's reception to welcome visitors to the first of the capital's festivities.

He wanted a woman who could function in formal settings and not be intimidated. From what he saw, it would take more than a mere monarch to intimidate the good doctor.

'The facility won't just help your country,' she continued, 'but the whole region. The medical research centre, with the funding you've announced, has potential to become a world leader.' She paused. 'And to have maternal and infant health as a priority area...' She shrugged. 'I could say it's far-sighted but I believe it's long overdue.'

She began to compare regional statistics for infant illness and life outcomes.

The doctor was outspoken but in this case for good reason. The need was great, especially as Salim's brother had removed money from the health budget to fund a pet project to design and manufacture luxury cars in Dhalkur. As the project had been inspired by enthusiasm rather than careful planning, it had died a swift, expensive death. Leaving Salim to make up the shortfall in medical services.

He admired Ingrid's focus. He needed a wife who could stand up for herself. The doctor, one of the women on Rosanna's list, combined brains, beauty and an air of competence that ticked several boxes.

Yet, as he listened, his gaze flicked across the room again to Rosanna.

She looked slender and understated in a dress of darkest green overlaid with a sheer layer of smoky grey that reminded him of the mists he'd seen rising off Norwegian fjords. There was an air of subtle enticement about her.

All night he'd been aware of her, as if some internal radar kept signalling her presence.

He'd barely seen her since that night in his rooms. When he made the mistake of touching her and she'd shied away.

As if she felt the same inexplicable connection and rejected it.

His mouth flattened.

Salim had been sensible and circumspect these last ten days. He'd kept their meetings to a minimum and always in his office rather than his private suite. But that didn't stop the buzz of awareness under his skin whenever he saw her or thought about her, which was far too often.

He'd only meant to pick up her laptop. Yet when his hand touched hers something changed. He hadn't consciously reached for her, but when his hand encircled her wrist and he felt that wildly fluttering pulse, it called to something just as wild in himself. Something untamed and primitive that didn't sit well with the self-contained man he'd trained all his life to become.

With his mother's early death, a busy father who had little time for his sons and a strict upbringing designed to make him a man who might one day rule the nation, self-denial was second nature.

That had been reinforced by life with a cruel older brother always ready to exploit signs of weakness or tenderness. Since returning to Dhalkur Salim had slipped back into ingrained behaviours, re-erecting personal barriers as easily as putting on clothes.

Salim never let emotions rule him. Not when his country needed his full attention. He was ever conscious of the need to prove himself more reliable, more serious and stable than Fuad, whose passions had weakened him and Dhalkur. The country needed him strong and focused.

Salim *couldn't* indulge himself with Rosanna. He'd hired her. The imbalance of power meant any approach by him would be sexual harassment. Besides, she was finding him a wife! What sort of man started an affair in those circumstances?

Yet he hadn't been able to banish that idea from his mind, no matter how he tried.

When he read reports he fancied he saw her sultry grey eyes on the pages. During long meetings he thought he heard her soft voice coaxing him to kiss her again. And at night…

'Ah, the intriguing Ms MacIain. It's good to meet you.'

Rosanna smiled even as a warning grazed the bare skin under the long, translucent sleeves of her dress. This man was trouble. His steely stare belied his greeting.

Dhalkur's Minister for Finance was powerful and reputedly eager for even more power, if the hints she'd heard in the palace's administration wing were to be believed. Taqi, Salim's assistant, was careful what he said but Rosanna suspected he wasn't a fan of the politician.

'I'm pleased to meet you too, sir. Though I fear I might disappoint. I've never thought of myself as intriguing.'

He nodded briskly before she'd finished even speaking. He definitely had an agenda.

'So what brings you here? Someone just pointed you out, saying you're working closely with our sheikh. But they didn't know what you're advising him on. Something personal, perhaps?'

His curiosity had an unpleasant edge as he leaned over her. Reflexively Rosanna stood taller, refusing to shuffle back when he tried to dominate her.

Was he jealous that someone else might have the king's ear? Or did he suspect the sheikh was seeking a bride?

Salim was adamant that their project be secret. He wanted no rivalry between powerful families. If they discovered he was choosing a bride, each would put forward their own candidate.

Fortunately Marian's company had a discreet online

presence with no staff names included. No one searching would connect Rosanna to a matchmaking business.

'As to that—'

A deep, smooth voice interrupted from just over her shoulder. 'Ms MacIain is a recruitment expert.'

The rich timbre of Salim's voice had an instant effect. Muscles clenched, heat swirled and the fitted bodice of her dress felt suddenly too snug. As if her breasts swelled. Now the brush of her dress against her skin felt like the caress of deft fingers.

Rosanna's thoughts fixed on that night when he'd touched her. He'd captured her wrist and she'd wanted, so badly, for him to tug her close and kiss her.

'Ms MacIain is assisting me with some personnel issues. But don't worry, I'm paying her myself, not taking funds from your budget.'

'Of course, Your Majesty. I didn't for a moment want to imply—'

'Of course you didn't.' Salim's voice held a note she couldn't identify. She wanted to turn and see his expression but it felt imperative to face this man and not risk showing her feelings for Salim. 'Ms MacIain has a degree in psychology and considerable experience in corporate management. Perhaps she might advise your department when she finishes assisting me. I hear there were irregularities…'

Rosanna bit her lip to stop a smile as the minister flinched then fixed on a wary smile, so different from his earlier, superior stare.

'I'm afraid circumstances were misreported. It was a trifling matter, soon dealt with.'

Minutes later, after a conversation about the sights Rosanna should see during her stay, the older man excused himself, claiming to see someone he'd promised to speak with.

'What was the problem in his department?' she asked softly when he left. 'He didn't like that one bit.'

Salim stepped forward and turned to face her. He looked tall, commanding and haughty. Every inch the powerful ruler. Yet humour lurked in his eyes and his mouth twitched in the hint of a smile that bathed her in the warmth of shared understanding.

How could that hint of expression, the tiniest indication of pleasure, affect her so profoundly?

Salim angled his head closer. 'Nepotism. My brother preferred important jobs went to those he favoured rather than those who merited it. Some in the government took their lead from him.' He shot a look to where the minister was talking gravely with a small group. 'I made it clear on my accession that favouritism wouldn't be tolerated. But some took a while to change their ways.'

'No wonder he didn't look happy.'

To a man who obviously valued his dignity and authority, the hint of a personal reprimand from his sheikh would be hard to swallow.

'He's rarely happy. I should have known he'd question you.'

'How so?'

Rosanna had kept in the background, working behind the scenes. Tonight was the first time she'd attended an official event and that was only because some of the women she'd suggested be invited to Dhalkur were here.

Salim's gaze moved past her as if checking if they could be overheard. 'He likes to know what's going on. Plus his niece is one of the women on your list.'

'She is? I wasn't aware of any family connection. How could he know? Only you and I—'

'Of course he doesn't know. But he's one of the senior government members pushing for a royal marriage so he understands the pressure on me to marry.'

'You think he suspects why I'm here?'

Salim's eyes met hers again and it was like colliding with a force of nature. That direct gaze seemed to penetrate deep inside, pinioning her to the spot and making her worry how much he saw of what she tried to hide. Her lungs squeezed tight. Deep in her pelvis heat blossomed.

Now his expression wasn't amused. 'I doubt it. He suspects you're here for completely different reasons.'

Rosanna tilted her head, trying to read Salim's expression. His chiselled features looked more pronounced, as if the flesh pulled tight across his face.

'You'll have to explain. I don't have a clue what you're talking about.'

One ebony eyebrow rose. 'Why might a man invite a beautiful woman to stay as a private guest in his home?'

It took a moment for Rosanna to digest his meaning.

She'd been distracted by the fact he'd called her beautiful. She wasn't and never had been that. She would have written off the comment as casual flattery, yet there was nothing casual about Salim now. She was close enough to feel tension emanate from him, a tension that tightened her own muscles and sinews till she felt at breaking point as his meaning sank in.

*The minister suspected she was the king's lover.*

She didn't know whether to be flattered or horrified.

'But that's—'

'Predictable? I admit I should have foreseen it.'

Stunned, Rosanna scanned the vast reception room.

But no one in the glamorous crowd was watching her in that superior, judgemental way the Minister for Finance had.

'He can't really think I'm an obstacle to his niece…' She paused, conscious that while they stood alone, it was better to be discreet. 'That I'm in the way.'

'You underestimate yourself. You're intelligent and engaging. And you look charming tonight.'

*Charming.* That deflated her illicit exhilaration at being thought the sheikh's lover. *Charming* was a word her grandma used when she couldn't find something more positive.

'In fact—' his voice dropped to a deep, mesmerising whisper '—I'm surprised you don't have a coterie of admirers swarming around. That dress was designed for seduction.'

'Seduction!' she yelped, then jammed her lips together.

'Don't act surprised. You must know you look ravishing.'

Rosanna opened her mouth then closed it again. Ravishing! The idea knocked her off balance. She'd never thought of herself in that way. Phil had never called her anything like that.

The cocktail-length dress had been a rare indulgence, purchased at a bargain price from an up-and-coming British designer grateful to Marian and Rosanna for their introduction to the suave Brazilian who was now her husband.

Rosanna loved the swish of satin as she moved and the deeply feminine style. She'd thought it elegant but demure, perfect for a formal occasion in Dhalkur. The dark green satin might have tiny shoulder straps and cling at the bodice and waist, but it fell in discreet folds from her hips and a sheer overdress of cobweb grey covered her bare arms and shoulders as well as the satin underdress.

'You think the dress seductive?'

'You have to ask?' Salim's eyes gleamed but not, this time, with amusement. 'The see-through cover just makes a man want to explore what's beneath, and the way it shapes to your body...' He shook his head. 'You're not naïve, Ms MacIain. You know exactly what effect you have on a man.'

*You.* Not the dress.

*Salim was calling her seductive.*

She shouldn't be thrilled but she was.

It had been a long time since Phil had made her feel desirable. Since then she'd been too busy trying to re-shape her life and put the past behind her to think about being sexy or desirable.

Except with Salim.

'I'm not going to apologise.' It wasn't as if she was showing excess cleavage. 'It's a lovely dress and I like wearing it.'

'I don't expect you to.' Yet he didn't smile and his voice sounded almost grim. 'It's time I circulated. I still have guests to greet.'

Rosanna followed his gaze to the other side of the room. The Scandinavian doctor she'd recommended as a potential wife stood among a cluster of attentive men. Clearly, despite what he just said, Salim wanted to return to her.

That was good news. So far he hadn't shown much interest in the other candidates, whereas the lovely doctor had obviously caught his attention.

Why did his interest niggle at Rosanna? It was positive, knowing she made progress, introducing him to a woman he found appealing.

*Because you don't want him attracted to the lovely blonde.*

*You want him attracted to you.*

Rosanna gasped and put a hand to her ribs as if that would still her knocking heart.

'Is something wrong?'

That acute gaze raked her and she felt abruptly vulnerable.

'No.' Rosanna scrambled for something to distract him. 'I just wondered how you knew about my psychology qualification.'

'You don't think I'd hire you without due diligence?' Reading her expression, he went on. 'No, I didn't have you investigated. Just the usual check of references. I don't do business with someone without ensuring they're able to deliver.'

Was that a reference to her lack of preparation when she came to Dhalkur? Or a simple statement of fact?

Either way it was a timely reminder that she was here to work, not fantasise about a relationship that could never be.

'Of course.' Rosanna stepped back. 'I'd better leave you before people think I'm monopolising you.'

Rosanna MacIain mightn't be monopolising his company but she'd taken over his thoughts. He spent the rest of the evening watching her from the corner of his eye. Even as he spoke to the women invited here for him to meet.

She'd chosen well. They all had qualities to recommend them and were all bright, self-possessed and attractive.

They were all blonde too, and at least topped his shoulder. Rosanna had taken those comments to heart.

He thought of her devoting her time to finding the perfect woman to meet his needs and the idea sent a forbidden thrill through him.

*Since she'd come into his life he had needs that it seemed only she could satisfy.*

He'd told himself his celibacy since taking the crown was to blame. But that was only part of the problem. The main part was Rosanna MacIain. Serious and conscientious. Intelligent and obstinate. Tenacious and effortlessly sexy. She even made a trouser suit look enticing. As for those soft lips and her give-everything brand of passion...

No wonder he craved her, waking nightly in a hot sweat, body throbbing with unassuaged need.

Dragging his mind back to the conversation around him, he congratulated one of Rosanna's candidates on her grasp of his language. She was a French diplomat who spoke five languages, had a throaty, attractive laugh and a love of the outdoors. She was also chic, sexy and engaging.

Theoretically they were an excellent match.

Yet, even as he leaned closer, telling her about four-wheel driving in the desert, his attention strayed to a dark head and a sensuous body in smoky green on the other side of the room.

Anger coiled in his gut.

Anger at Rosanna and at his wayward inclinations.

This wouldn't do.

He didn't have the time or inclination to drag out his search for a wife. The sooner it was sorted the better. But Rosanna MacIain was proving as much a hindrance as a help, distracting him at every turn.

She was surprisingly good at her job. Surprising because at heart he'd never quite believed a matchmaker could find a woman he'd consider marrying. She'd proved him wrong, producing several candidates who might fit the bill.

*If only he could concentrate on them and not her.*

Either she had to go or he had to find a way to neutralise her hold over his libido.

# CHAPTER SIX

'Your Majesty.'

Rosanna kept her voice even despite rising frustration. Despite his delay acknowledging her amongst the throng waiting to speak to him at the museum opening. He only deigned to recognise her because she refused to move away.

His congenial smile solidified as the other guests melted away.

He inclined his head briefly, his tone as cool as hers. 'Ms MacIain.'

What had happened to the man who, at last week's royal reception, had called her beautiful and seductive? Whose dark gaze had made her feel more feminine and alluring, more *alive* than she'd ever felt in her life. He'd even come to her aid when the Minister for Finance had grilled her.

But Salim had only intervened because he didn't want the secret of her work getting out. It had been nothing to do with Rosanna herself.

Strange how his indifference hurt. She felt it as a crushing weight in her chest and a ridiculous prickling behind her eyes. That made her angrier still.

Rosanna tilted her jaw, her gaze locking with his. This wasn't about her. It was about her work, and *noth-*

*ing*, she vowed, would stand in the way of her delivering what she'd promised.

Not even a client who refused to see her.

Every meeting she'd tried to organise had been cancelled except for a brief quarter of an hour with his assistant present. It was as if Salim didn't want to deal with her.

'We need to talk.'

'Indeed?'

His expression didn't change, yet the look in his eyes reminded her that she spoke to an absolute ruler. A man used to instant and complete acquiescence.

'If you please, Your Majesty.' Rosanna made her voice soft and coaxing but she was damned if she'd bow her head or break eye contact now she finally had his attention. 'I need to update you and I can't proceed without your guidance.'

Because, despite producing a selection of gorgeous, talented women, Salim didn't seem interested in any of them. Not even Ingrid, the Scandinavian medico with the grace of a queen and the looks of a film star.

At this rate Rosanna would be here for months.

She shuddered. She had to pin him down and get him to spend more time with the ones he liked best.

Was he deliberately sabotaging her work?

But that made no sense. Salim had made it clear he needed a wife quickly, even if he acted like a man who would prefer not to marry.

'I'm sure my assistant will be able to—'

'With all due respect, Your Majesty, it's you I need to speak with, not your assistant.'

If Salim had looked proud before, now he was positively imperious, staring down that aristocratic nose

as if she were the first person who had ever interrupted him.

Perhaps she was. Anxiety curdled her stomach as she
thought of the consequences of displeasing this powerful client.

'I was about to say—' he paused as if challenging
her to interrupt again '—that my assistant will make
an appointment.'

He looked up and instantly Taqi hurried towards
them.

'Thank you, Your Majesty. I'll look forward to it.'

Rosanna suspected her smile was more like a baring
of teeth, but her patience was fraying, especially with
Marian calling regularly from London asking for progress and Salim refusing to give enough useful feedback.

'Excellent.' He was already turning away with Taqi
in tow, leaving Rosanna to wonder what she'd done to
earn his displeasure.

But she'd had difficult clients before. She vowed that
not even the Sheikh of Dhalkur at his most regal and
uppity would get the better of her.

'Ms MacIain, Your Majesty.'

Late that same afternoon Salim watched Taqi usher
Rosanna into his sitting room then leave, closing the
door behind him.

Salim rose from the sofa where he'd been reviewing
a report, silently cursing his earlier distraction.

He'd come to his private apartments to search for
notes he'd made last night on a new project and become
absorbed comparing them with the progress report he'd
received. When he hadn't returned to the office, Taqi
must have assumed he was happy to meet Rosanna here.

*Not* what Salim had intended. It felt safer meeting her in the administrative wing, with his staff nearby.

But surely such a precaution wasn't necessary. He could hear her out and send her on her way.

'Please, come in.'

His voice was half an octave lower than usual and seemed to rumble from somewhere far deeper than his larynx.

Her voice, by comparison, was crisply uninflected. 'Thank you.'

She still wore the dress of cobalt blue from the museum event. Less severe than her work clothes, it skimmed her body in a way that made Salim's throat dry. Even the sight of her slender legs felt like too much temptation to a man battling for control. Like a teenager instead of an experienced man of the world.

A mighty shudder rippled down Salim's spine.

A portent of trouble? Or anticipation?

Her chin was up and her gaze direct, as if ready for a confrontation.

*Was that the real reason he'd come to his rooms and stayed here?*

*Because he knew their relationship teetered on the brink of something perilous.*

*Perhaps, subconsciously, he courted that danger.*

Salim's pulse slowed to a heavy thud as he battled the urge to reach for her and see those gunmetal eyes glitter silver with desire.

That would be a monumental error. He wasn't a man to be undone by physical urges, no matter how compelling. Even if he knew that he wasn't the only one feeling this way. Rosanna might pretend to be untouchable but she hadn't been able to hide completely her response to him.

Salim's life had been a lesson in self-mastery and strategic focus. Spur of the moment impulses, giving in to selfish desires, weren't encouraged in royal princes. That had been his brother's style, which was one of the reasons he'd been passed over as sheikh and Salim, the dependable, hardworking brother, had been chosen.

He didn't feel dependable now. He felt...

'Please, take a seat.'

He gestured to the long sofa opposite before sinking back onto his own.

As soon as she sat, in a sinuous movement that notched his temperature higher, he realised his mistake. They should be at a desk, a very wide desk where Rosanna would be safely on the far side out of reach and those shapely legs out of his line of vision.

Although she sat with her knees together and ankles demurely crossed, her dress rode distractingly higher and Salim had to concentrate on not staring.

He cleared his throat. 'You had matters to discuss.'

She did. Lots.

Rosanna had been busy, which is what he'd come to expect. She had a slew of new candidates for him to consider. A proposed schedule which would allow him to meet them at upcoming events. Plus her observations on the women to whom he'd already been introduced. All detailed, all insightful, all logical.

Yet Salim couldn't focus on the meeting's desired outcome. Moving closer to choosing a bride.

Finally she paused, looking at him in expectant silence.

'You've done well. I can see why your aunt's enterprise is so successful.'

'But?' She looked at him, eyebrows raised and lips pursed. 'I hear a *but* in there.' She drew a slow breath as if searching for calm. 'We don't seem to be making progress. You need to be open with me about your responses to these women. Then we can move forward and find the right one for you.'

*I've already found her.*

The thought jammed his tongue and stopped his breath for a second.

Not as a wife. Rosanna MacIain didn't fit those criteria.

Fuad's unstable, selfish temperament and his excesses while ruling for their ailing father proved how the wrong person in a royal role could damage the nation. Even a well-meaning but unprepared person would flounder. Salim needed an absolute paragon as a wife. A woman with an unblemished past who wouldn't undermine the royal family's prestige but help him rebuild it. A woman with the unique mix of skills and experience that would make her a superb queen.

Yet Rosanna was the woman he wanted for *now*.

That was the problem. With Rosanna in his home it was impossible to think about other women.

His mind and body betrayed him by continually focusing on his stern, sexy siren. Replaying the passionate kiss that had been a promise of carnal pleasure. Even her tight control and prim corporate suits only emphasised the alluring dichotomy of a capable woman whose businesslike exterior hid sultry ardour.

'I need your frank thoughts on the women you've met. Otherwise, how can I tailor my search to your requirements?'

Dark pewter eyes held his and he read determination there. Unfortunately he still yearned to see them silver with passion.

He shot to his feet and stalked to the window, looking out onto the city, fighting the adrenaline surge in his blood. Every muscle tightened, ready for decisive action. As if he weren't a modern monarch but one of his ancestors, men famous for taking what they wanted and negotiating later.

Salim breathed deep and kept his gaze on the rooftops, turning bronze and gilt as the sun waned. 'What do you want to know?'

'Who would you like to see again? There are limits on getting to know people in formal settings. In a more relaxed atmosphere—'

'None.'

'What? You don't want to spend time with *any* of them?'

He turned and saw her composure had cracked. Her mouth hung open for a second until she snapped it shut.

Her eyes sparked fire and, despite his best intentions, Salim felt satisfaction curl deep inside. He liked watching Rosanna flare up like that, even in anger if he couldn't have anything else.

He disliked it when she hid all that passion. Even if it was the correct, cautious thing to do, the sort of thing he was trying to do himself. It felt like fraud.

Salim put his hands behind his back, standing taller, knowing he was on dangerous ground. He felt it in every pore. As if he'd wandered into a treacherous bed of quicksand that looked innocent but could devour an unwary man.

When Rosanna spoke her voice was perfectly modulated. 'It would be helpful, Your Majesty, if we could go through each one and you told me why they weren't suitable.'

They were back to *Your Majesty*?

He shouldn't be surprised. He'd called her Ms Mac-

Iain today, careful to observe the formalities in public. But it had been more than that; he'd been angry with himself, and with his feelings for her. He'd done all he could to avoid being alone with her.

*Face it, Salim. You were running scared!*

It was a first for him. One he didn't like.

So he'd snapped at her. Done his best to distance himself at the museum, channelling his brother at his most haughty. Yet it hadn't worked. He'd still wanted her.

'As you wish. Run through the list.'

'Right then. Let's start with Lady Charlotte.'

'She's allergic to the Dhalkur.'

'Sorry?' Rosanna goggled at him. 'How can she be allergic to a country?'

'When we drove to the edge of the desert she was worried about getting sand blown into her hair. Plus she fretted that such a dry climate would dehydrate her skin.' He watched Rosanna's expression grow horrified.

'I'm so sorry. I had no idea. She sounded so good on paper, and when we talked. She didn't mention anything like that.'

Rosanna frowned, clearly blaming herself for not picking that up earlier.

'It's not the sort of thing you could discover from a search.' Yet that frown didn't shift. He let his mouth curl. 'She did assure me that she functions perfectly as long as she has twenty-four-hour air-conditioning.'

Salim watched a ripple soften the line of Rosanna's flattened lips. Then he heard a gurgle of laughter.

He felt it like a trickle of heat winding through his body, leaving him even more aware of the fact they were alone in his private space. 'You weren't to know.

I expect she deliberately kept some things to herself until she got here.'

She shook her head and made a note. 'How about Jazmin?'

'A lovely woman and on paper she met my criteria. Especially with her first-hand knowledge of the region.'

'And in person?'

'Even though she's cousin to a king and grew up at his court, she confessed she's not comfortable with formal events. She's happier mixing with people in the country than at official receptions. That won't do for my wife.'

Rosanna sighed. 'Another who wasn't quite straight with me. I do apologise.'

She looked so downcast Salim felt sorry for her. She'd worked hard and done a good job. But he was determined to take only the right woman as his bride.

He needed someone who could hold her own in both formal and informal settings. Someone who could appear soignée yet welcoming at formal functions.

His thoughts strayed to Rosanna in misty green at that recent reception. She'd been beautiful and assured but engaging. He'd seen her talking animatedly with many of his guests and wished he could join her.

But even an outsider as confident as Rosanna would find it impossible to adapt a royal life full-time. He needed someone whose family circumstances or training equipped them for the demands of royal life. He'd spent a lifetime preparing for it and still sometimes his new position felt overwhelming. As if, just for a short space, he craved the chance to be simply Salim, not the ruler everyone looked to for solutions and leadership.

Salim snapped his mind away from fruitless thoughts. 'Who's next?'

'Princess Eliana.'

'No.' He saw Rosanna open her mouth ready to protest and raised his hand. 'She's pretty and clever and
probably very nice, but she finishes my sentences. Do
you have any idea how annoying that is?'

'I—'

'Very annoying. I couldn't live with someone who
did that.'

'I'm amazed she had the temerity.'

Salim stared at Rosanna with her downcast eyes and
nimble fingers making yet more notes. Was she laugh-
ing at him?

But even Rosanna's snarky observation was nothing compared to the frustration of having someone put
words into his mouth.

'I don't mind a spirited conversation.' He drew
himself up. 'But not someone pretending to know my
thoughts.'

'No, of course not.'

Yet he read the smile lurking at the corners of her
mouth. To his chagrin he felt his own mouth curl. His
was a valid complaint yet Rosanna made him see the
amusing side of it.

'What about Ingrid—'

'The doctor,' he said flatly. He'd had hopes of the
beautiful, aristocratic Scandinavian, but they'd been
deflated. 'Definitely not.'

'It would help to know why. She's beautiful, talented,
presents well and speaks several languages.'

Salim shrugged. 'She's totally focused on her research.'

'You said you admired women who pursued careers.'

'Not to the exclusion of all else. Whenever someone
raised a subject that wasn't to do with her specific area

of interest she listened politely but had nothing to say. I want a wife who's interested in people, makes them feel welcome.'

'I'm sure if you gave her another chance…'

Salim shook his head and turned back to the window. 'No. I've made my decision. She's not the woman for me.'

'Okay then. What about Sylvie? She's got the diplomatic and linguistic qualifications you wanted and is very capable.'

Salim shook his head. 'She won't do. All the time I was with her I felt like I was being assessed so she could tailor her conversation to fit. I could almost hear the wheels turning in her mind.'

Rosanna didn't say anything and her silence eventually made him turn to look at her. She was looking across at him, frowning, her mouth a flat line.

'That's unfair. Of course she was thinking about what might interest you. She was trying to get to know you.'

'It was more than that. It just felt too…contrived. She lacked spontaneity.'

When he'd met Rosanna, for instance, their conversation had been easy and entertaining and felt as natural as water bubbling from a mountain spring.

Rosanna's frown didn't shift. 'So conversation is important. You want someone who talks easily and is interested in a lot of subjects.'

Put like that it sounded very basic, but that was precisely what he wanted. 'That's right.'

'So, then there's Natalya.'

'No sexual spark.'

Rosanna's eyebrows shot sky-high. 'Sorry?'

'She's a nice woman, I'll give you that. She's friendly

and intelligent and not at all fazed by life at court, but I wasn't attracted to her.'

'But she's a model. She's the face of a multi-million-dollar cosmetics campaign!'

Salim shrugged. 'She's beautiful. But not for me.'

For some reason her ice-blonde beauty didn't move him. He'd spent several hours with her and felt not the least stirring of sexual awareness.

Whereas, he realised, he just had to be in the same room with Rosanna MacIain for his libido to throb into life. He set his jaw, determined to get this over. 'Who's next?'

They dealt with several more on her list. Salim's answers grew shorter and Rosanna's mouth tighter as she noted his objections. Everything from shyness to an annoying, high-pitched giggle, to one who'd tried to seduce him at their first meeting and whom he labelled too pushy.

Rosanna drew a slow breath and made yet another note. She looked grimmer than ever.

'So, you want a woman who's aristocratic, preferably royal, or used to mixing in such circles. She must be beautiful, but in a way you can't specifically describe. She has to be confident but not too confident. Able to satisfy you sexually but not be sexually predatory. You'd like a competent, career woman but not so focused she isn't interested in other things. She needs to be able to talk with anyone, but not presume to put words into their mouth. Someone who's at home in a formal setting but not just there. She must have a sense of humour and warmth but not an annoying laugh or any sort of verbal tic. Plus she has to like Dhalkur, be an accomplished linguist with not a whiff of scandal about her and be eager to have children.'

Salim nodded. 'Excellent. You've described her well.'

As he watched, Rosanna pinched the bridge of her nose and squeezed her eyes shut. She drew a deep breath then busied herself making another note. But she didn't raise her eyes to his.

'Right, what about Maryam, the last woman you met? She meets a lot of those criteria.'

Salim was already shaking his head. 'On paper she seems right, but in reality...' He paused, remembering those big doe eyes looking up at him. 'She deferred to me all the time. Even when I asked her a straightforward question she was reluctant to commit herself in case it wasn't the answer I wanted.'

'With respect, Your Majesty, that's not surprising.' He didn't miss the snap in Rosanna's voice, as if she held her temper by a thread. 'You can be quite daunting.'

'I told you to dispense with my title in private.' The way she said it, as if it tasted sour on her tongue, irked him. Or maybe it was the judgemental way her mouth flattened as he gave his completely legitimate reasons for each rejection. 'As for your *with respect*, that's what you say when you're feeling not at all respectful.'

She met his eyes, her stare fulminating. Yet she retained her composure and said nothing. Salim realised he was trying to crack the barrier she'd erected around herself. She challenged him yet pulled back at the final moment.

That was a good thing. It was safer that way, for both of them. Yet it frustrated him.

He wanted more from her.

'If you feel you're not up to the job...'

'Are you sure there really *is* a job?' She set aside her laptop and stared up at him, her gaze probing.

He frowned. 'What are you talking about?'

'Your requirements keep changing and expanding. I bring you one of the world's most beautiful women and you claim you don't find her attractive.'

'I didn't say that. She is attractive. I just don't *want* her.'

Because, infuriatingly, his body and mind were fixated on Rosanna MacIain. The knowledge made him grit his teeth in annoyance. He was lord of all he surveyed and the one thing he wanted was the one thing he shouldn't want. Because she was his guest, his employee...

And the source of more frustration than he'd ever felt in his life. When he was with her he didn't feel like a king or her employer. He felt like a man lost in the desert, thirsting for a single taste of pure, lifegiving water.

'Are you playing some sort of game?' Emotion coloured her voice. She sounded fed up. 'Are you sure a tall, blonde aristocrat will meet your needs—'

'Why, Ms MacIain? Do you think a medium height brunette from Australia might be a better fit for my needs?'

Her gasp was loud in the thrumming silence. She shot to her feet, eyes flashing pure silver, hands curling into fists beside her. 'If you're implying—'

'I'm not implying anything, just pondering.'

And, despite his better judgement, enjoying the fact she was no longer treating him like a professional challenge. He much preferred her honest emotions, though he wouldn't accept such insolence from anyone else.

The air sizzled with the energy she radiated. Salim felt it like a shower of sparks peppering his skin. And in the heavy weight settling in his lower body. The strain of clenching muscles.

'I'd never…' She shook her head as if words failed her, but not for long. 'No, *you're* the one sabotaging this process. *I'm* the one trying to keep it on track.'

She dragged in deep breaths, her breasts rising against her blue dress. Valiantly Salim refocused on her face, flushed and vibrant.

'That's the problem. This project isn't on track at all. It's going off the rails.'

It was his fault for agreeing to have her here. He should have known better that night when she'd stalked into his office as if she owned it, demanding to know what he was doing there. That stirring excitement hadn't left him since. He'd been on tenterhooks, trying to do the right thing, curbing a reaction to her that was as undeniable as it was inconvenient.

She hiked up her chin, at the same time cocking her hip and planting her hand on it in an attitude of pure, feminine provocation that was impossible to resist.

'Okay. I'll bite. Why, in your opinion, is it going off the rails? Tell me straight. Don't waste any more of my time.'

'Why? Because of this, of course.'

Salim took a single stride that brought him right up to her. He saw her narrowed eyes widen but not, he saw, in dismay. He slipped one arm around her waist, drawing her against him, and cupped the back of her head with his other hand.

For an instant he was lost in the white-hot flare of light in her eyes, then he bent his head and his mouth met hers.

# CHAPTER SEVEN

ROSANNA HAD SENSED the kiss coming in the static charge that made every hair on her body stand up. In the elation that had ramped up the longer they were together. She'd *seen* it coming, Salim's head lowering towards her in slow motion as if daring her to push him away.

Yet she hadn't done a thing to avoid his kiss.

She hadn't turned her head or pushed him back or said a word in protest.

How could she when this was exactly what she'd craved all these months?

Instead she'd grabbed his shirtfront and watched, breathless, as those dark eyes came closer and she tumbled into their midnight depths.

Finally, as his lips covered hers, it hit her. The most overpowering relief. As if she'd waited all her life for this moment.

Despite the energy running through her, Rosanna sagged a little, knees giving way and legs trembling with reaction. All because she experienced again the taste of his mouth on hers. As if she'd hungered all this time for the indefinable flavour that was pure Salim.

But even that weakness brought its reward as his hard frame pressed against her, his hold enveloping her, and joy burst free.

Salim's fingers moved, pulling her tight bun free and channelling through her hair in a bold caress that was sumptuous and delicious.

Almost as bold and delicious as the way he kissed, knowing and satisfying, yet full of promise.

They were like lovers parted too long. Lovers who knew each other intimately. Salim *did* know her intimately. The stroke of his tongue, the angle of his mouth and the hard but not too hard pressure aroused and captivated her. As if he knew exactly what she wanted.

Rosanna squirmed closer, pressing herself against him, revelling in the contours of his body, his powerful thighs wide around hers. And all that glorious heat.

Salim caressed her scalp, gently tugging her hair so her head tilted backwards, giving him better access, and she couldn't prevent a muffled groan of pleasure.

Instantly his grip around her waist tightened, pulling her so close she registered his arousal, potent against her abdomen.

A shiver ran down her spine and across her skin. At her core was a melting sensation as if she softened, ready for his possession.

Yet, kissing him back, her hands tugging him closer, Rosanna didn't feel weak or overwhelmed. She felt as if she'd met her other half. As if they were designed for each other in some elemental way.

This was how she remembered that night in Scotland. Pure passion, the promise of wonderful things to come, the sense of union between like souls and a sheer carnal arousal such as she'd never known.

Salim lifted his mouth and Rosanna almost cried out in dismay. Except he wasn't moving away, just giving her a chance to breathe while he peppered kisses to the corner of her lips, her jaw, then the spot just below her ear that made her jerk in his arms and press closer, hunger reaching impossible levels.

'Salim!' Was that keening, breathless voice hers?

He said something deep and low in a language she didn't understand, his lips brushing her neck, his hot breath a caress that sent a quiver of longing through her.

He straightened, glittering eyes holding her in thrall. 'You want me to stop?' His voice hit a harsh note.

'No!'

Rosanna blinked as her instinctive denial sank in. They teetered on the brink of something far bigger than a kiss and they both knew it.

'I…'

She struggled for something to say. To remember all the reasons this shouldn't happen. But while her brain was scrambled her body was awake and too, too responsive. Salim drew a deep breath and that movement created friction against her breasts. Her nipples were tight, hard and needy and she wanted him to touch her there.

Rosanna gulped.

*Madness, this was madness.*

'Madness or not, it feels right. You can't deny that.'

Rosanna stared. She'd said it out loud?

'This is why our search isn't working,' he went on, his voice a gravel rumble. 'Because all I can think about is you, Rosanna.'

The way he said her name, his voice dipping, made something unravel inside her.

Or was it the way he held her, with an easy possessiveness that she shouldn't like yet revelled in? Then there was the way he looked at her. Gone was that haughty superiority, replaced by searing intensity and an honesty that cut through every common-sense reason to keep her distance.

Or perhaps it was the stunning import of his words.
*All I can think about is you.*

She soaked that up like a flower absorbing sunshine.
Greedily. Delighted to discover she wasn't alone in this
forbidden longing.

'We can't,' she mumbled, her throat closing convul-
sively as desire waged war with professional ethics. 'I
work for you.'

Salim straightened, his head rearing back, his hold
loosening though he didn't relinquish her. 'You think
I'm pressuring you to—'

Rosanna stopped his words with her fingertips to
his mouth. Arousal ran through her at the feel of his
lips against her skin. Reluctantly she dragged her hand
away. 'No! Not that. This isn't harassment. Nothing
like it.'

This was utterly consensual and she couldn't pretend
otherwise. 'But I have a job to do. I have to find you—'

'At this moment I don't care about finding a bride.'
His low voice held a savagery she'd never heard before
and it sent a thrill through her bones. Never had she felt
a man's need for her like this. Not even the man she'd
once planned to marry. 'All I want, all I've wanted for
weeks, is you.'

His hands moved, gathering her closer. Rosanna
knew she only had to step back and he'd release her.
But that act of will was beyond her. She stood trembling
not from fear or outrage but from excitement.

What did that say about her?

*That you need him just as much as he needs you.*

The discovery that their longing was mutual swept
away all the arguments she'd used to tell herself there
couldn't be anything between them but a contract of work.

It changed everything.

Her heart hammered and her breathing turned shallow. Her head spun with Salim's cedar and spice scent and the feel of his body, primed yet waiting for her answer.

'I can't think about other women. I can't concentrate. I'm continually struggling for control because every time I see you, even when I *can't* see you, I'm fighting the urge to do all the things I know I shouldn't... with you.'

'Really? But today—'

'Today I was in a temper. I apologise for being so short with you. I shouldn't have taken my foul mood out on you and I'm sorry.' He scowled and, instead of deterring her, it made something in her chest roll over as she sensed his internal battle. 'I've tried keeping my distance and not see you alone but it makes no difference. I'm not used to being unable to control my reactions.'

'*That's* why you refused to meet me?'

It threw a whole new light on his actions.

Salim nodded grimly. 'Much good it did me.'

He sounded sulky, like a man used to getting his own way and suddenly discovering he couldn't. For some reason Rosanna found that almost endearing. Or maybe it was just the confirmation that he too had suffered.

Salim shifted his weight and the brush of hard muscle against her body made her feminine core tighten needily.

'I want you, Rosanna.'

She watched him swallow, his Adam's apple jerking and the muscles in his bronzed throat working. The movement emphasised both his strength and the extremity of his tension. It made her feel suddenly strong, a *femme fatale* wielding seductive power. Except the power flowed both ways. Everything about Salim called to her, making her weak with longing.

'I need you.'

Even then he didn't plead but stood proud and tall, like a warrior of old.

Rosanna squeezed her eyes shut. Her imagination was on overload. She did *not* need to start imagining his as some romantic hero of the desert, swooping in to claim the woman of his dreams.

'Rosanna?'

His arm dropped from around her back and her eyes snapped open in dismay. He was releasing her?

That's when it truly struck her. That despite the pair of them together being a terrible idea, the alternative— to walk away—was impossible.

'I need you too.'

She hadn't meant to say it, but looking into those dark velvet eyes the truth just tumbled out.

Rosanna saw him absorb her words, not with a smile but with a clenching jaw and flared nostrils. Far from leaning in to scoop her closer he seemed to straighten still further, towering above her.

Never had she been more conscious of his power, of the fact that he was all hard, male muscle, honed by his desert heritage and military training into a force far stronger than she could ever be.

Yet that didn't scare her. It thrilled her. For the look in his eyes, hunger melded with something she couldn't name, told her he wouldn't use that power against her. It was himself he battled.

The knowledge, sudden and sure, made her feel like a different woman, as assured as a queen, any doubts fading to nothing.

She lifted her hand, intending to caress that clenched

jawline, but he moved faster, long fingers wrapping around her wrist before she could touch him.

'Not here.'

His voice was thick, almost unrecognisable, but Rosanna understood, because she felt the same. They needed absolute privacy for what was to come. Because one touch would lead to another then another…

Rosanna's breath hitched and a smile trembled on her lips.

Did she imagine his eyes dilated? Before she could be sure, he turned, still holding her wrist, stalking away from the window. They passed groups of sofas and occasional tables, heading for a door on the far side of the room.

Salim's stride didn't seem hurried but Rosanna took two paces to each of his, her pulse ratcheting faster with each step and each hasty indrawn breath.

Through the door they passed a book-lined study on one side and what looked like a media room on the other. They swept past a gym that gave out onto a courtyard with a massive swimming pool. Past a couple of closed doors and finally through double doors into his bedroom.

Salim paused to close the door behind them yet didn't let her go.

Heat encircled her wrist and a shivery feeling of euphoria shot through her, tinged with just the tiniest bit of trepidation.

Rosanna wanted Salim more than she could remember ever wanting anyone or anything. Yet such intensity of feeling was outside her experience.

The snick of the door shutting them in his private domain was as loud as a gong echoing through the silence.

Rather than look at Salim she focused on the high,

domed ceiling, painted the colour of the sky just after sunset, azure darkening to indigo at the top. She just had time to register a sprinkling of silvery stars against the blue when Salim led her forward.

Two large, elegantly arched windows gave views towards distant mountains. Between them stretched an embroidered coverlet of blue and gold, covering the biggest bed she'd ever seen.

Her breath caught in a gasp she couldn't prevent.

Moments ago she'd thought of Salim as a warrior of old, stern and uncompromising, sweeping his chosen woman up and away. This massive bed perfectly fitted that desert fantasy.

'It's a bit over the top, I admit,' he drawled near her ear, 'but it's tradition and it's comfortable. A new one is made for each new sheikh.'

'Imagine trying to launder the sheets.' Rosanna's voice sounded stretched. 'It must be a nightmare.'

She snapped her mouth shut, realising she was babbling. The enormity of this moment thickened her breathing and revved her heartbeat to a staccato rush. She didn't dare look at Salim.

*In case he sees how profound this feels for you?*

*Or in case he changes his mind?*

He'd said he needed her and she felt the same. But out of nowhere, doubts assailed her. Rosanna wasn't gorgeous or gifted. She didn't speak five languages or heal sick children or negotiate international trade deals like the women Salim had rejected. She was ordinary, so ordinary that her ex had needed more in his life, dreaming of a glamorous life beyond their means.

Salim's thumb stroked a tiny circle on the pulse point at her wrist, making her shiver. But instead of taking her in his arms and kissing her, he stood beside her, radiating heat and that delicious spicy scent of warm male flesh.

'I confess, I've never thought about it,' he said, 'but I suppose you're right. I don't think I've thought about laundry since my days doing national service, washing my own clothes.'

'You washed your own clothes?' She turned to find him watching her, his expression unreadable.

'Naturally. Even the son of the sheikh gets no special treatment when it comes to doing his duty. In fact, I'm sure my father instructed that the year's military service should be as taxing as possible. He believed in toughening his sons to meet future challenges.'

Salim paused, his expression enigmatic. 'Is this too much of a challenge, Rosanna?' His voice dropped, the sound scraping through her, proof again of her visceral response to him. 'Have you changed your mind? You seem nervous.'

This was her chance to back out. Because it didn't make any sense, her with a man like Salim.

But that was the old, hurt Rosanna trying to wrest control. The one bruised by what Phil had done and crushed by guilt over his actions. The Rosanna who doubted too easily and second-guessed her judgement.

She didn't want to be that Rosanna any more. It had been testing, but she'd revelled in the stimulation of her work for Salim and the chance to prove herself. She liked feeling competent and strong.

*She liked the way Salim made her feel.*

Rosanna nodded. 'I am nervous.' She'd never had sex with anyone but her ex-fiancé, but that would be too much information. 'I don't…share myself easily or often.'

'Neither do I. There's been no one since before the night we met in the Highlands.'

Rosanna's eyes rounded. She hadn't expected that. A man like Salim could have his choice of eager women.

She thought of all the things she might say. Except if she opened her mouth now she didn't trust herself not to babble out more inanities. Besides, it wasn't talk she wanted.

Rosanna turned to face him, planting her free hand on his broad chest. Feeling the quickened thud of his heart beneath her palm eased her tension a little, because it proved he was nowhere near as sanguine as he appeared.

She splayed her fingers and leaned in. 'Kiss me, Salim. I don't want to talk any more.'

His mouth curled into a smile that stole her breath all over again. 'Your wish is my command.'

Rosanna caught the indulgent humour in Salim's eyes as he deliberately played into that fantasy, and suddenly her nerves dissipated. She was grinning up at him as he gathered her close and kissed her with a deliberation that left no room for second thoughts.

She wanted him. *How* she wanted him.

Her fingers scrabbled at the tiny buttons on his collarless shirt even as she lost herself in the sensual exploration of mouth on mouth, of bodies straining together, eager for more.

She felt Salim lift one hand at the back of her dress, then the slow, tantalising slide of the zip that was a caress in itself. She arched against him, eager for more.

'Drop your arms, sweetheart,' he murmured against her mouth and she felt strong fingers wrapping around her wrists, pulling her hands to her sides. Moments later her dress pooled around her ankles, leaving her in underwear and high-heeled sandals while Salim was still fully clothed.

Rosanna kept her gaze on his face as he captured her hands again and drew them wide, away from her body. He looked down, surveying each swell and dip with an attention so exquisitely sharp she felt it like the skim of fingers across bare flesh.

She might have felt uncomfortable under that scrutiny, like some slave girl being inspected by a potential buyer. Except she *wanted* this with every particle of her being. Besides, watching Salim through half-closed eyes, she registered the dusky heat slash across his high-cut cheeks. Saw the convulsive swallow and felt the needy way his hands tightened on hers.

He said something soft and low that sounded like treacle poured over grinding stones. The unfamiliar words were lush and rich yet harsh with emotion as if his larynx had seized.

Then ebony eyes met hers and something heavy swooped inside her. 'You're stunning, Rosanna.'

A tiny part of her brain told her Salim must be as desperate with need as she was. She'd never been called stunning and she knew she was average. Yet she responded unthinkingly to the accolade, standing taller, breasts swelling and nipples budding so tight the ache almost made her cry out.

'I want to see you too.'

She didn't consciously form the words but suddenly they were out and she was glad.

Salim released her hands but not her gaze as he made short work of a couple more buttons then hauled his shirt off. It was incredibly arousing, having him watch her as he undressed.

Finally, though, she had to follow the movement of his hands downwards.

Her breath stalled on the sight of a honed body that seemed all lean strength. The shift of muscles beneath golden skin mesmerised her. The dusting of dark hair across his wide chest invited her touch and she found it surprisingly silky and tempting beneath her fingertips.

A gasp filled the silence but whether it was from Salim or her she didn't know.

Was there anything in the world as wonderful as the feel of hot, sculpted, male muscle twitching against her touch?

Salim's hands dropped to his trousers and Rosanna's eyes widened. In what seemed like one urgent shove he dispensed with the rest of his clothes and his footwear as well, leaving him utterly naked.

Rosanna blinked, her mouth drying.

She'd never seen such male perfection. Had never thought to in real life. Salim's tall body was perfectly proportioned with wide shoulders, narrow hips, solid thighs and a jutting erection that made that soft spot low in her body turn molten. Even his bare feet were sexy.

But it was the invitation in his eyes that stole her breath. That and the little flare of his nostrils that told her he too struggled for control.

'Come.' He held out his hand palm up in invitation. She put her hand in his and instantly long fingers encircled hers, drawing her to him.

Now she was surrounded by his heat, soaking it up eagerly, pressing closer, kissing his collarbone and throat. He tasted of spice and salt with a deeper note that was intrinsically, excitingly, pure male.

So entranced was she that she barely noticed him

remove her underwear until they stood, naked flesh to naked flesh, and it felt as if her body sang out loud.

In one easy movement Salim lifted her then lowered her to the bed, following her so fast she was cocooned between his hot body and the silken coverlet. The sensations were so delicious it was a sybaritic overload. Desperately she stroked his bare body, shifting against him, revelling in the friction between them and the fascinating new delights.

Salim kissed her again, as easy as a long-term lover and more thrilling than anything she'd known.

Rosanna lifted her hands, channelling her fingers through his thick hair to cup the back of his skull. She shifted her legs wider so he sank against her, all magnificent heat and shockingly potent arousal.

'Please,' she whispered against his mouth. 'Please, Salim.'

Sex had never felt like this before. With Phil she'd never known this out-of-her-mind urgency. Never this sharp pang of need as if she'd die if she didn't join with Salim soon.

She lifted her hips, tilting against his erection, and it felt so good. Her breaths came in gasps and the fire in her blood concentrated where their bodies met.

Salim moved, his weight shifting to one side, and Rosanna felt his hand on her body. But instead of going straight to her breasts as she expected, those long fingers delved, down her abdomen and lower, following her slick heat to the cleft that hid the centre of her need.

Rosanna shuddered as electricity jolted through her, emanating from the press of his fingers against her clitoris. She snapped open eyes she hadn't realised she'd closed to see Salim watching her, gaze intent, his mouth taut and his breathing as harsh as her own.

She opened her mouth to say she wanted more than his touch. She wanted all of him. But he stroked her again, circling that sensitive bud, rubbing harder then deeper, testing her slick channel. Her pelvis rose of its own volition, drawn by a power stronger than thought.

His gaze held her captive as he lavished her with words of encouragement, urging her to let go.

A cry choked off her breath as everything within Rosanna coalesced into a single shining burst of energy. It was shockingly sudden, so quick she scarcely believed it. She felt it rise and expand, her blood sizzling, flames licking her bones, and joy, stunning and incandescent, consumed her.

Her taut body collapsed, boneless and weightless, and her eyes drifted shut, her brain overloaded by pleasure.

Salim moved away and dimly she assumed he was getting protection. Rosanna stretched languidly, her body buzzing still. Soon he returned. She felt the bed dip beside her then furnace heat as satiny flesh slid against her.

'Thank you,' she whispered.

'You're very welcome.'

How could that warm, husky voice sound so arousing after her monumental climax? She opened her eyes and felt instantly guilty that while she lay relaxed and sated, Salim was on edge. She saw it in the bunched muscles of his shoulders and the razor-sharp lines of his jaw and cheekbones, as if his flesh had been scraped to the bone.

'Salim.'

His name was magic on her lips as she reached for him. He settled between her legs, taking some of his weight on his arms. His erection felt impressive against her inner thigh but Rosanna didn't feel nervous, despite a relative lack of experience. She wanted to give him pleasure such as he'd offered her.

She wrapped her arms around him, lifting her mouth to his.

'Take me,' she whispered against his lips. 'I want to feel you come inside me.'

She might have lit a fuse on dynamite.

One moment Salim was holding himself back, as if concerned not to rush her. The next she heard and felt his deep groan of need as he kissed her hard, pressing her down into the pillows. He kneed her thighs wide then, with a single sure thrust, slipped in right to the heart of her.

Rosanna gasped, her breath failing as she struggled to absorb every delicious sensation. She'd never felt so full. So intimately connected to another. As if she hovered on the brink of some secret world, hitherto unknown.

'Rosanna. Did I hurt you?'

She shook her head. 'No.'

Her brain worked furiously, suddenly awake after that blissful lethargy. It told her these feelings were due to simple physics. That Salim was bigger, in all respects, than Phil. Plus he'd already given her an amazing orgasm, whereas, in the past, she'd struggled to climax. That had to explain why this union felt so profoundly different.

'Open your eyes, Rosanna.'

She did and it felt as if she fell into black velvet. Could Salim's eyes actually be so dark? Just looking at them excited her. As for breathing in his rich, addictive scent and feeling his body against hers…

'I need to be sure you're okay.'

A cracked laugh escaped her lips. 'I'm more than

okay. I'm... I don't have the words.' Because even this, just lying together, joined, felt utterly miraculous.

Still he didn't move though that was what she craved. Rosanna lifted her legs, winding them over his hips, hugging him to her and feeling him slide even deeper.

She felt a quiver ripple through Salim, felt his muscles bunch, and a second later he withdrew and thrust again.

Rosanna's head pressed back into pillowy softness as she arched up to him, his name a raw gasp on her lips. Her hands clutched, nails digging into cushioned muscle as she felt, impossibly, arousal stir anew. Tendrils of heat unfurled and twined through her, tightening at each erogenous zone.

Salim thrust again, deeper and more emphatic, and his hand closed around her breast. In the past when Phil had caressed her there it had sometimes been nice but often he'd squeezed too hard, too eager to read her body well as he sought his own relief. Salim's touch wasn't like that. She wanted more of it, more of everything.

'Like that?' His voice was gruff, almost unrecognisable, and she loved it. Loved knowing he too was on the edge.

'Exactly like that.' Rosanna struggled to find her breath as their bodies arched and thrust together as if they weren't virtual strangers but long-term lovers. 'Please,' she gasped. 'More.'

Something flared in Salim's eyes. His tempo quickened and his movements grew less measured, as if he too felt that primal beat in his blood. Rosanna met him, thrust for thrust, caught up in that surging tempo, until it burst upon her, an explosion of rapture that carried her to a place she'd never known.

She heard Salim shout her name, a long, deep groan

of completion so raw it sounded almost like pain. Her climax should be dying but the quick, insistent pulse of his ejaculation drew her muscles into spasm again and her brain into paradise.

Rosanna felt utterly, wonderfully complete.

# CHAPTER EIGHT

SALIM DISPOSED OF the condom then doused his head under the cold tap, trying to shock his brain into action. He stood, arms braced on the bathroom counter, head sunk between his shoulders, trying to think.

It had never been so hard to concentrate. His thoughts kept straying to Rosanna, luscious and inviting in his bed, so unconsciously seductive.

Unconsciously? He was imagining things.

Yet while she was innately passionate, Rosanna Mac-Iain wasn't a practised seductress. More than once he'd caught her look of surprise. At her loss of control? At her multiple orgasms?

That was his ego talking. Wanting her to be blown away by how good they'd been together, as if no other man had made her feel anything comparable.

Salim's rueful smile died on his lips.

*It was true. That's exactly what he wanted.*

He lifted his head and looked in the mirror. A frown corrugated his brow and the lines carved around his mouth spoke of tension, despite the lingering echoes of bliss in his body.

Because no matter how good sex with Rosanna had been—and it had been phenomenally good—it had also been a mistake.

He employed her. It went against every rule to mix business with his personal life. Even though it had been consensual, he was her boss and he didn't like the disparity in power.

Salim's mouth rucked up in a wry grimace. Now he was sheikh there would always be a disparity in power between himself and any woman, wouldn't there?

His situation had changed so much, and though his upbringing had been designed to prepare him for such a possibility, the change sideswiped him sometimes.

He needed to be careful, behaving with decorum as well as decency. The example set by his brother, of reckless enthusiasms, inconsistent and questionable decision-making and personal cruelty, still lingered in the public psyche. Salim was doing his utmost to reassure his people that he wasn't like Fuad.

His brother's enthusiasms hadn't run to women but to fast cars, high-stakes gambling and a never-ending series of expensive whims. He'd siphoned funds earmarked for public programs to his private, lavish expenditure. As a result, Salim was particularly cautious of any actions that hinted he put his personal interests ahead of his duty.

Plus Salim had always kept his sexual liaisons private. In the days when he'd lived part-time in his father's palace and part-time elsewhere, he'd never invited a lover here, and there'd been no lovers since he took the throne because the needs of his nation had come before his own.

*Because there was no woman you wanted as much as the stranger you left behind in the Highlands.*

His mouth flattened in response to that truth. It made him restless and uncomfortable. Because, even now he'd had her, he still wanted Rosanna. Too much.

On every level he could think of, sex with Rosanna MacIain had the potential for disastrous consequences. It was wrong, or it should be wrong.

*Yet it felt utterly right.*

The glow of wellbeing that suffused his body and clouded his brain was testament to that.

Salim scowled at his reflection. He needed a solution to the problem that was his yearning for this woman.

She was here to find him a spouse. How could he expect her to continue now they were sexually involved? Even considering it made something sour roil in his belly, as if he were being unfaithful to a woman he hadn't yet met. Or to the woman who'd just shared his bed.

Yet he'd committed to the search for the sake of his people who had been through so much in recent years. He didn't have the luxury of choice. He *couldn't* turn back now.

How could he proceed while his thoughts were filled with Rosanna? When he hadn't had a full night's sleep in weeks because of his craving for her?

There had to be a solution. And he had to find it *now*.

Rosanna heard Salim get out of bed then the snick of a door closing.

Her breath escaped on a sigh that was part bliss and part wonder. She'd never felt like this in her life. Boneless, weightless and buzzing with absolute pleasure.

She'd been engaged, had been with Phil for a couple of years. Yet what she'd just shared with Salim was totally new territory. She felt wrung out, her body well-used and exhausted yet at the same time trickles of rapture still coursed through her and a sense of absolute rightness filled her.

Salim had taken her to places she'd never known and brought spectacular, unrivalled joy. He'd called her *sweetheart* in a way that had melted her heart. He'd given her tenderness as well as shockingly raw carnality. She felt like a different woman, sexy and powerful as never before.

And conflicted.

The smile curving her lips faded as the real world crowded in. The world beyond this vast, decadent bed.

Rosanna opened her eyes and saw afternoon light slanting across the room, picking out the gold embroidery on the rich coverlet. It was daylight and she was lolling on the sheikh's bed.

Would staff come looking for him? What if he had more meetings? Or if not, would they bring refreshments to his rooms?

She had to leave before she was seen.

Yet, with her body lethargic from bliss, she found it hard to move.

Dazed, she lay there, telling herself she'd move in a moment, when she gathered strength to stand. Staring up, she realised the stars on the ceiling weren't some painted, regular pattern. They sparkled like gemstones, and instead of being in neat rows, they were scattered across the vast space in what she realised now was a star map showing constellations she'd seen in the night sky.

The sight distracted her. That someone had taken the time to create a virtual starry night especially for their sheikh was amazing. And that they'd done it with…no, surely they weren't real gems…

That thought brought her back with a thud to reality. Naked and ravished to within an inch of her sanity by Salim, her body gently throbbing from his possession. No wonder she was grinning again.

Except Salim wasn't simply the man she'd yearned for. He was trouble. A client. A king. Surrounded by watchers and commentators. A man who could snap his fingers and have whichever woman he wanted.

What had she been to him?

Rosanna wanted to believe she was more to him than an afternoon's indulgence, but that would be a problem of monumental proportions. Neither of them was suited to an affair. Salim because he was searching for a wife. Rosanna because she wasn't into short-term flings. This was her first. A liaison had the potential to wreck her mission here and through that both her reputation and her aunt's business.

She snatched in a sharp breath that caught between her ribs. She catapulted off the bed then paused a moment, knees trembling and heart pounding, but she couldn't afford to linger. Hurriedly she stumbled forward, snatching up her crumpled dress. A puddle of gleaming anthracite grey silk caught her eye and she lunged for her underwear near the foot of the bed.

Where was her bra? And her shoes? Had they been kicked under the bed?

She was hunched over looking for them when warm fingers shackled her wrist. Instantly she froze.

'Not so fast, Rosanna. Where do you think you're going?'

Slowly she straightened, her pulse quick and high in her throat. Excitement stirred but she struggled to fight it, knowing she couldn't afford to be dazzled again by carnal enticement.

Rosanna turned and there he was, looking even bigger, more handsome and imposing than when he was fully dressed.

She fought the urge to forget common sense and lean

against him so he could gather her close. She wanted
the comfort of Salim's body wrapped around hers so
she could ignore for a little longer the harsh realities
that faced her.

'I'm going to my room, after I find all my clothes.'

His raised eyebrows told her he hadn't expected that.
'You think you can just walk away?'

That superior stare cut through her dazed thoughts.
It was a timely reminder that her exciting, wonderful
lover was an autocratic ruler, used to having everything he wanted.

Including women?

The idea dimmed Rosanna's lingering joy. He'd convinced her that he too had been affected by their meeting in Scotland. That he'd been fighting their attraction.

Yet how well did she really know him? Her track
record with men was terrible. She'd trusted Phil and
planned a future with him but he'd turned out to be
nothing like the man she'd believed him. He'd made a
mockery of her vaunted skills at sizing people up.

Rosanna swallowed hard. Maybe, despite what Salim
had said, she'd just been convenient.

She straightened, tossing her hair over her shoulder,
trying to ignore the fact they were both naked and that
her traitorous body was stimulated by having him so
close. She tugged at his hold but he didn't let go.

'Of course I can walk away if I choose. I'm not your
possession. I'm not here for your convenience. If I want
to leave that's my choice.'

Her stare dared him to disagree.

Salim released her and held up his hands, palms towards her as if emphasising that she was free.

The trouble was she didn't feel free. She felt bound
to this man in ways she couldn't even begin to name.

'If you go, where will that leave us? With nothing resolved, that's where.' He paused as if to ensure she took in every word. 'You still want me, Rosanna. I know you do. And this cuts both ways. I want you too. What we shared has only increased the wanting.'

Her pulse hammered faster, her breathing turning fast and shallow. Salim felt the same. Stupid to feel pleased but she did.

'If you walk away now we'll still have the same problem. We can't keep our hands off each other even though this is the last thing either of us wants.'

*Well, that was her told.* Rosanna's pleasure dimmed.

Maybe her hurt showed for his expression softened. 'Come, sit with me. We need to talk.'

He bent to reach for his discarded clothes and Rosanna's tongue stuck to the roof of her mouth as she watched the mesmerising movement of his honed body.

He held out his shirt to her. She took it in stiff fingers, watching as he yanked on his trousers, not bothering to do up the top button, then sat on the side of the bed and patted the mattress beside him.

Rosanna breathed deep, drawing in the scent of exotic spices, of lemon soap, warm male flesh and sex. It was a heady mix, so heady she knew he was right. He was impossible to resist. This attraction was too strong and she had no idea how to fight it.

Even if she wanted to.

Her dress dropped to the floor as she put his shirt on, doing it up with trembling fingers then rolling up the sleeves. It covered her yet she was supremely aware of her nakedness beneath the fine cotton. Strange that after what they'd just done together, she felt overwhelmed by the intimacy of wearing his clothes.

Carefully she sat beside him, striving to keep her gaze off his bare torso.

Salim nodded encouragingly. 'This has crept up on us both. The connection, the desire, and it's so strong it feels unstoppable.'

Rosanna was taken aback by his frankness. She was simultaneously gladdened and scared because if they were both weak in the face of this attraction, where did that leave them?

She wasn't naïve enough to believe this could end with flowers and promises of happy ever after. She and Salim came from different worlds with different expectations. Their paths would only cross for a brief time.

She could never be the sort of woman he needed and even in her wildest dreams she couldn't imagine living in a grand palace. Yet the thought of walking away from Salim tore at something vital inside her.

Rosanna had a job to do but this, between them, was a devastating roadblock.

'I tried to resist,' he continued. 'But keeping my distance and throwing up barriers didn't make a difference. Nor did the fact that you've been the epitome of efficiency and productivity. It made me wonder if you were trying to distract yourself from us too.'

The way he said that one syllable, *us*, with a deep scrape of his baritone, sent a shiver of longing through her.

He twisted towards her and suddenly he was touching her, the lightest of caresses, a single finger stroking the underside of her forearm, yet Rosanna felt it like an earthquake, shattering the foundations of her world. She trembled, her nipples puckering towards him and a ribbon of heat swirling through her core. Her lips parted and she had to stop herself from leaning closer.

'I don't think either of those tactics will work again, do you?' His voice was soft, sneaking beneath her tattered defences and winding around her heart. 'Even if you're superefficient and focused and I try to avoid you or treat you like a stranger, the truth between us is too big. We've let the genie out of the bottle and there's no way to push it back inside and pretend it doesn't exist.'

That light touch skimmed down to her hand, circled her wrist then slipped across her palm and a great shudder of longing racked her. Just that tiny caress and she needed him. She swayed towards him then caught herself and sat straighter, yet she didn't have the strength to pull away.

'So,' she finally managed in a voice turned uneven with emotion, 'if we can't go back to being strangers, how do we go forward?'

Salim's hand closed around hers and he nodded, a half-smile forming on his face. 'I like that you don't waste time in pointless argument,' he said. 'That you're always looking ahead to what needs to be done.'

It was the sort of accolade Rosanna was used to hearing on a professional front. It was something that had stood her in good stead in the commercial world. Now though, Salim's compliment felt personal.

It made her realise how much she craved positive reinforcement, after the tough time she'd had back home in Australia. Her family had said she'd taken on too much personal blame for events she couldn't have prevented. She didn't agree. But maybe she'd been too hard on herself since such a simple compliment felt so important.

'Thank you. And I like the fact *you* don't prevaricate. You say what you're thinking.'

Even though his straight talking sometimes tested

her patience, like when he found fault with every one
of the women she'd brought to Dhalkur.

But how would she have coped if he'd taken a shine
to one of them? Rosanna tried to imagine herself watching him woo and possibly seduce another woman and
her stomach tied itself in knots. Something sharp jabbed
her chest, twisting deep, and she had a horrible feeling it
was jealousy. For something that hadn't even happened!

'So you want me to be straight with you?'

'Of course.' This was no time for guessing games.

Salim nodded. 'We can't go back to the way we were
and the way we are now—' his hand tightened on hers
'—isn't sustainable long-term. Agreed?'

'Agreed.'

Because if this relationship continued long-term it
would make Rosanna his mistress. The idea was anath-
ema to her. She had no desire to be a convenient lover
on the side, especially when he married. Rosanna respected marriage vows and hoped one day to find the
right man with whom to spend the rest of her life.

She'd thought Phil was that man. Her disillusion-
ment at her mistake had put her off dating ever since.

'Then I can think of only one solution. We become
lovers for a short time.'

Salim's thumb stroked across her wrist and onto her
palm, creating ripples of erotic delight that made her
breath stall. Or was it the idea of being his lover?

'How will that make a difference? It would just com-
plicate things.'

Nausea churned in her stomach. She couldn't imagine working daily to find his perfect spouse then spending each night in his bed.

'We'd have to put your work on hold. It wouldn't feel
right, continuing that while we shared a bed.'

Rosanna looked into his sternly sculpted face and felt relief flutter through her with each heartbeat. Relief and enthusiasm at the idea of them as lovers.

She'd wondered if he shared her scruples. It was good to hear that he did. The thought of finding him his perfect match while they were intimate had a distasteful edge to it. As if she really were some disposable mistress and what they shared meant nothing to him.

'I'm glad you feel that way. I couldn't do this—' she gestured to the lavish bed '—and be your matchmaker at the same time.'

Strange that it hadn't even occurred to her to say no to becoming his lover. But Rosanna wasn't into self-delusion. She couldn't turn her back on this, no matter how she tried. He was right, the genie was well and truly out of the bottle. How much harder would it be, being around him, trying to work, when all the time her thoughts were veering to sex?

'It would be wrong to ask that of you. I've already found it too tough trying to do justice to the women you've brought forward while my thoughts are focused on you. It feels deceitful both to them and you.'

Rosanna put her hand over where he held hers. 'Thank you, Salim. I've been tying myself in knots over this. It's a relief to know you have the same concerns.'

Their eyes met and something powerful passed between them. Understanding. Relief. Respect. All that and more.

Slowly his taut features eased into a hint of a smile that sent warmth easing through her. 'So we're agreed. Now we just need to do something about it.'

Rosanna didn't miss the eager glint in his eyes. 'But I don't see how an affair will solve our problem.'

'It's the only solution. We have a short, intense affair and this attraction will burn itself out.'

'But will it? How do you know?'

He tilted his head as if to read her expression better. 'It's what always happens with an affair. Passion and fun and pleasure, then it fades and we move on.'

'Really?'

'Of course. Surely you've found the same.'

Rosanna thought of not answering but this was too important. Besides, it wasn't anything to be ashamed of. 'I've never had an affair before so I don't know.'

Shock showed in those dark eyes and his hand tightened reflexively around hers. 'But you weren't a virgin.'

It was a statement, yet she heard the echo of a question there.

She shook her head. 'No, but I was in a long-term relationship. I'd planned to marry and in the meantime...' She shrugged.

There was silence for a moment. 'So you've only been with one man before me?'

Salim looked so serious, so surprised, almost as if he'd never heard of such a thing, that Rosanna fought a smile. 'What can I say? I've always been more interested in finding a man I can love rather than someone for a short fling. It's not a crime, you know.'

He blinked and sat straighter as if suddenly realising how close he'd leaned towards her. 'Of course not. I admire you.'

'But that's not your experience.'

'Searching for love? Never. Until now sex without commitment has been enough for me.'

Well, she'd wanted honesty. Rosanna opened her mouth to ask if he expected love to grow in his marriage, then thought better of it.

'And from your considerable experience, you believe that if we have an affair, this—' she waved her hand in an encompassing gesture '—will burn itself out?'

Perhaps she was naïve but it didn't feel like something that would disappear fast. But then she was a novice, she had discovered, to such extreme sexual pleasure. She'd have to rely on Salim's expertise.

'Definitely.'

He sounded absolutely certain. That was a relief, though a tiny part of her almost regretted it.

'Good. That's good to know.'

'You don't sound convinced.'

She shrugged and looked away. 'You're right that we need to move on. But at the same time I rather liked…'

'Oh, so did I, Rosanna.' His voice ground to a rough note that ran through her middle like suede brushing sensitive skin, making her quiver. When he spoke again there was a hint of amusement as well as a definite promise in his tone. 'But don't worry. There will be plenty more pleasure before we're finished, I can absolutely promise that.'

Her head snapped around and their eyes met. What she saw in his expression made her chest grow tight and her body soften.

Rosanna swallowed hard, trying to appear calm despite the heat flushing her cheeks and the suddenly altered atmosphere. Was it a new scent in the air? A thickening weight to the momentary silence? Or the burgeoning excitement through her whole nervous system as she fought not to lean into him and offer her lips to his. She was aware of the air caressing her skin with each breath she took, of the sensitivity in her breasts, belly and lower still that spoke of arousal.

It wasn't just a kiss she wanted. Sitting half-naked next to Salim was torture. She wanted to touch him.

Wanted that powerful body moving with hers, the sound of his breathing hoarse in her ear as he came, and took her with him into ecstasy.

'You're doing it again,' he growled.

'Doing what?'

'Looking at me the way you did before. Like you want me to ravish you.'

*Yes, please.*

But she didn't say it, because her mouth had turned desert dry at the gleam in his dark eyes.

'How long will it take?'

'Sorry?' He looked startled and she couldn't blame him. Dragging her mind back to the thread of their conversation was almost impossible.

'This affair. How long till we can…conquer this?'

'Ah. The time frame for our affair.' Did he move closer or did she imagine it? 'I'd like to say a month but I don't have much time available. What we need is to be together day and night, sating ourselves. A stolen hour here or there just won't do it.'

Rosanna took a slow breath and nodded, trying not to look shocked at the prospect of *sating themselves*. It sounded decadent and intoxicatingly tempting.

'I suggest a week.' His eyes held hers as if daring her to disagree. 'A week where we'd be totally alone.'

Rosanna couldn't help it, she shivered in pleasure at the prospect.

What was happening to her? This was totally outside her realm of experience, yet instead of being shocked or hesitant, she couldn't wait.

Rosanna moistened her dry mouth with her tongue. 'When?'

Salim's attention lifted from her lips and she was thrilled to read arousal in his hooded eyes.

'As soon as I can manage it. I'll get Taqi onto it

straight away. It will take a little time to reschedule everything and clear my diary so we can go away together.'

'We're going away?'

'Definitely. We want absolute privacy for what I have in mind. Only one or two people whom I trust absolutely will be aware that we're together. That way we can protect your reputation and not give rise to gossip.' He paused. 'Does that sound okay?'

More than okay. The fact that he wasn't just considering the need to slake his desire, but aiming to protect her privacy, meant a lot.

In many ways Salim had the qualities Rosanna appreciated in a man. He was thoughtful as well as decisive and he cared about others. From what she'd gathered his decision to choose a bride was prompted by the need to allay others' fears over the lack of an heir. He took his responsibilities seriously.

'You think it will solve our problem?'

'I do.'

'Then,' she admitted, 'I think it's a great idea.'

The only difficulty would be trying to keep up the appearance of professionalism in the meantime.

'Excellent.'

He looked like a man who'd just sealed a great deal.

Suddenly Rosanna felt uncomfortable, sitting here, calculating how to have an affair. She wanted it yet at the same time she felt…

*What do you expect? To be swept into his arms as if the world didn't matter? To be wooed with promises of happy ever after?*

Instantly a metal wall clanged down in her brain.

No more false promises. No more hazy romantic daydreams. This was the real world.

She slipped her hands from Salim's and wrenched her gaze away too. She found herself looking down at her bright blue dress, discarded on the floor. She still had to find a way back to her room without anyone seeing her looking as if—

'It's time I left. I'll get my clothes and go.'

As she watched a large hand covered hers. 'Soon. But there's something we need to do first.'

'What's that?'

Rosanna made the mistake of looking up. Her pulse stuttered as she read the heat in Salim's expression and the curling smile on his lips.

'We need to seal our deal.' He paused, then lifted her hand, skimming his lips over her knuckles and watching as she tried and failed not to quiver. 'After all, it could be days and days, not to mention long nights, before we're alone again, Rosanna. I think we deserve a little indulgence now to keep us going. Don't you?'

Salim leaned close, one hand on her shoulder, and she found herself lying on the bed looking up into that hard, handsome face, all thoughts of leaving disintegrating.

Beyond him a shaft of dying daylight hit a constellation of stars on that beautiful, indigo ceiling. A reminder that she was totally out of her depth, playing dangerous games with a powerful royal in a world she didn't fully understand.

But none of that mattered as Salim undid the buttons on the shirt that covered her and straddled her hips. When his mouth found hers Rosanna sighed and clutched him close. Time enough to worry about it all later.

# CHAPTER NINE

'HE'S A DIFFICULT client then,' Marian mused.

'Hmm.'

Rosanna's reply was noncommittal as she shifted on the seat of the rose-covered arbour in what she thought of as her private courtyard. The warmth of the day lingered, producing a honey-rich scent that urged her already relaxed muscles towards torpor.

A day after that life-altering afternoon in Salim's private rooms and she still felt the aftereffects. She'd gone there impatient at his determination to find fault. But after his confession that *she* was the reason he couldn't focus on the beautiful women brought before him, it was hard to remain angry.

'You don't think he's difficult?' Marion sounded surprised.

'He certainly knows what he doesn't want,' Rosanna said carefully. 'But as well as choosing a life partner he's picking a consort. She will have to be someone quite special to fulfil those royal duties.'

The more Rosanna saw of Salim's work and responsibilities the more she appreciated he had to choose wisely. Especially with the country's traditionalists trying to direct his choice.

For the first time she found herself feeling sorry for those born royal. He couldn't simply choose for himself.

'That's a relief,' Marian interrupted her thoughts. 'I was afraid you might feel overwhelmed by the task. Not because you're not up to it,' she hurried to explain. 'But because it was always going to be difficult.'

'You knew that? Why didn't you warn me?'

Rosanna thought of the hours she'd spent second-guessing herself, wondering how she could have done better.

'I didn't want to scare you. Especially as it was your first solo effort since I'm still stuck here. I've only done one royal match but I remember how tough it was. It wasn't just the bridegroom who had to be satisfied but his family and any number of powerbrokers in the kingdom.'

'I'm sure Salim will make the final decision.'

'Salim? You're on first-name terms? That's a good sign.'

Rosanna was grateful her aunt couldn't see the guilty heat climbing her cheeks.

She thought of what she'd been doing this time yesterday in Salim's bed and had to draw a calming breath. He'd led her back to her room via a private passage, one that went directly from his suite to the cluster of apartments in what he'd informed her used to be the harem.

She'd been both horrified and thrilled at being led along a route made solely to give the ruler easy access to the women's quarters. She was thankful it saved her from being seen by palace employees in her crumpled clothes. But it reinforced the disparity in power that had always existed between the sheikh and his lovers.

*Now she was one of them.*

She was torn between illicit excitement and dismay.

That hadn't stopped her disappointment when he'd led her to her room, kissed her hand in a courtly gesture of dismissal and disappeared the way they'd come. She'd hoped he'd make love to her again and through the night she'd found herself looking at the concealed door, wondering if it might open and he'd come to her.

The fact that he hadn't had made Rosanna wonder, once more, if he needed her as much as she needed him. When she'd agreed to an affair she'd felt empowered. Yet now she felt uncharacteristically unsure.

She grimaced. Her experience with Phil had knocked her confidence more than she'd thought. Either that or this attraction to Salim was more powerful than she'd imagined.

'Rose?'

She gathered her scrambled wits. 'He's only formal in public. But it doesn't make him any easier to please.'

That was a downright lie, she realised. Sexually they were very attuned indeed and she'd pleased him very easily.

'Sheikh Salim has to be particularly careful in his choice. My sources tell me the country was troubled while his brother governed for their ill father. There were whispers of power abuses and shady dealings. The country even came close to war with its neighbour Nahrat until the Nahrati king married Sheikh Salim's cousin.'

'I didn't know that.' Rosanna had heard about the previous king and his elder son who'd acted as regent when he became ill but not much more.

'Ah well, I have my sources.'

She sure did. Marian's insider knowledge of the rich and famous was second to none.

'And those sources tell you there's pressure on Sheikh Salim?'

Strange how protective that made her feel. As if she could do anything to protect Salim!

'Absolutely. He's trying to get the country back on track after the damage his brother did. That would be part of the reason he needs a wife with no scandal in her past. He'll also need a woman who can hold her own in a traditional country as it modernises.'

Rosanna's curiosity about Salim's brother grew. The man was dead but his shadow lingered. It wasn't in her remit but Rosanna couldn't help wondering how Salim's odious brother had affected him personally. The man she knew was capable, focused and at times arrogant but he seemed remarkably level-headed.

'Now,' Marian said. 'Run me through his preferences again so we can consider how to broaden our field.'

Rosanna moistened her lips, her self-consciousness growing. 'Salim is planning a break. He's going to take a week off and doesn't want to be bothered with matchmaking during that time.'

He'd been adamant that while they were together he didn't want even to think about other women and that suited her completely. She paused, trying to still the telltale wobble inside. Her aunt was a clever woman and would grow curious if Rosanna sounded nervous. 'I thought I'd take a few days off at the same time. See something outside the palace.'

Rosanna held her breath. She had a wonderful relationship with Marian and part of her yearned to confide in her and seek her advice. Except she feared she knew what Marian would advise. That she leave Dhalkur and Salim immediately. No matter how much she loved and respected her aunt, Rosanna couldn't do that. Not yet. Not while she felt this way about Salim.

'Excellent. A short break will do you good. But all the more reason to review our progress now.'

For Salim the days since that afternoon with Rosanna dragged.

Because he'd made himself keep his distance, knowing that if he didn't there'd be no keeping the secret of their liaison. While his reputation wouldn't be affected, he didn't want her embarrassed.

So that afternoon, against every personal inclination, he'd led her to her room then left, despite the shimmering invitation in her eyes.

He hadn't seen her since.

That had taken more determination, more stoicism in the face of physical discomfort, than his whole year of military service. He was on fire with wanting her. His body grew more taut and cramped by the day as his unrelieved tension built.

He'd known it would be impossible to take a break immediately. A royal schedule wasn't easily cleared. But his patience wore thin as the days passed, each seeming longer than the last. The nights longer still.

Usually he had so much to do that the days were too short. Before he'd become sheikh he'd kept a hectic schedule, seeking out and developing international partnerships that could benefit his country. He'd been away on one such mission when his father took ill.

Since taking the throne he'd been busy, not merely with the normal business of the country, but undoing the morass his brother, Fuad, had made of the public finances and taking steps towards the changes he wanted to make.

Which meant every day was packed with meetings, paperwork, consultations and public events.

Yet now they dragged.

Had his father ever felt like this? Strung too tight and distracted because of a woman? It was hard to imagine.

Salim missed the old man. They hadn't always seen eye to eye. His father had been cautious about many innovations Salim wanted to pursue, but he'd been a decent, dedicated man.

He'd have appreciated his father's perspective right now.

Grimly Salim laughed and opened the last document before him. His father wouldn't approve of his son making time for an affair with a foreigner when he should be choosing a spouse. His father had been a great one for ensuring the stability of the nation. Even Salim, who had no desire for a wife, knew it was imperative that he marry and start a family. He'd seen how dangerous instability could be and understood the mood of his people.

But the thought of wife-hunting made him feel sick in the gut. The only woman he could think of was Rosanna.

He glanced towards the window. The sun would be up soon and he wanted to finish his work before taking Rosanna to their secret rendezvous.

His pulse quickened as anticipation stirred.

Finally they could be alone. A whole week with her beckoned. He couldn't recall ever feeling such elation at the prospect of being with a woman.

Maybe the anticipation was heightened because these days he was so hemmed in by court traditions and royal rules. Because he was no longer a private citizen.

Yet ever since the night he'd met Rosanna something had felt different.

Salim shoved aside such notions and read through the document to appoint a High Court judge. He signed with a flourish then added it to the pile.

As he sat back and rolled his stiff shoulders, he caught the first glimmer of grey lightening the eastern sky. A smile broke across his face. It was time.

Rosanna hunched into her jacket as the four-wheel drive sped along the highway, grateful that she'd known enough to understand that a desert could get cold at night.

Not that it was cold in the air-conditioned vehicle, yet her skin prickled as if from the dawn chill.

'You're warm enough?'

Salim didn't take his eyes off the road but he was attuned to her. Rosanna didn't know whether to be pleased or disturbed by that.

'I'm fine. Besides, it will be warm when the sun's up.'

'True, but not as warm where we're going as in the city.'

She nodded, hoping the casual clothes she'd packed would be suitable.

Who was she fooling? The way Salim had looked at her as he invited her into the vehicle made her wonder how often she'd get to wear clothes at all. His dark eyes had been as black as ebony. Just as when he'd made love to her. Despite the morning chill she'd felt distinctly overdressed. And delighted.

Rosanna focused on the road rather than the man beside her. For the first time since they'd met she felt close to being tongue-tied. That worried her. He might be a king but she was her own woman. She couldn't afford to be cowed by Salim. He already dazzled her too much.

'It's glorious here.' She swallowed, her throat dry. 'The mountains look wonderful in this light.'

The dawn light painted the peaks in a wash of gold turning to apricot, the deep clefts a dark indigo that made her think of the beautiful ceiling above his bed.

Her mouth lifted in a crooked smile. Clearly she had a one-track mind around Salim.

'I'm glad you think so. Dawn and dusk are my favourite times in the desert.'

'You come here often?' There was a moment's silence then they both laughed. 'That sounded so stilted. I'm not sure why when I'm interested in the answer.'

Salim lifted one hand from the wheel and placed it briefly on her denim-covered thigh. Instantly heat radiated from his touch and she shivered at the delicious sensations.

'I know why. You're nervous.' Rosanna frowned, about to deny it, when he added, 'So am I.'

'You are?' She forgot her determination not to watch him and twisted in her seat, taking in his proud profile as he put his hand back on the steering wheel. 'What have you got to be nervous about?'

He was the one with all the experience. She was the novice when it came to an affair.

He knew the place they were going. They were in his territory. She was the outsider.

More, he looked the epitome of calm control. Just as he did whenever they met in his office or at some function.

Salim shrugged and for the first time she registered that the movement didn't have its usual fluid ease. As if his shoulders were stiff.

'That you'll change your mind about this. Why do you think I'm breaking the speed limit to get there?'

His voice was light yet there was something about it that sounded like truth.

She glanced at the speedometer. 'You're not speeding.'

He shot her a smile that undid her and left her glad she was sitting down. She knew her legs wouldn't support her after that loaded grin.

'Not now because we're turning off the tarmac.'

On the words, he slowed and took a fork onto a gravel road that wound around a low hill. There was no evidence of a town ahead, not even a signpost marking the road.

'Where, exactly, are we going?' She'd imagined everything from a nomad tent to a vast, modern home. 'Wherever it is,' she said as the vehicle bumped over a dry gully, 'it doesn't look like they encourage visitors.'

'We don't.'

He sounded smug.

'We?'

'The royal family. This is our private road. Only the locals and our security staff know about it. It's not on any maps.'

'And it takes us where?'

The mountains ahead looked wild. Maybe they were going to camp in a cave. Though that didn't seem a good venue for a week of decadence.

'Up there.'

She followed his pointing hand towards the foothills of the mountain range. Tucked in the curve of a ridge, perched above a ravine, she saw a blob of pale pink. As they drove closer she made out straight lines and realised it was a building, though it seemed to grow from the natural rock.

'What is it? It's too big for a house.'

'It's the Queen's Palace and it is, actually, a house, albeit a fortified one. Don't worry, it's comfortable. The royal family has been using it as a private bolthole for generations.' He paused. 'I've known the caretakers all my life. They're utterly discreet so you don't have to worry about news of your presence leaking out. They won't come inside unless we send for them. We can be utterly private.'

There it was again, that note of complacency in his deep voice. Rosanna was glad they'd be alone. That's what she craved. Yet she couldn't prevent that tiny tremble of nerves.

She wanted to be with Salim. There was no question of that but she wondered if this scheme would cure her infatuation. What if an affair only cemented it? Strengthened it into something more than lust?

The thought scared her into speech. She didn't care if she was babbling, she had to break the silence and her thoughts.

'But it's pink. Is that because it was designed for a queen? It doesn't look like a place a sheikh would choose for a getaway.'

A chuckle rolled across her skin and loosened her clenched muscles. 'You think it's not macho enough for fearsome desert kings?' He shook his head. 'It's made of pink granite, one of the strongest local materials, and I can tell you it withstood at least one siege. But over time it was redesigned from a fortress to a private retreat. It's known as the Queen's Palace and the royal family comes here for pleasure.'

Did she imagine the way his voice dropped on the

word *pleasure*? Or the connection between pleasure and the sheikh's consort?

It seemed to Rosanna that all those dry reference texts describing the power wielded by hereditary Dhalkuri sheikhs should include a note specifically about them as dangerous seducers.

Salim only had to drop his voice to that baritone rumble, or unleash a sexy chuckle, and she turned to mush.

How would she fare after a week in his company?

She told herself she was doing the right thing. That at the end of their week they could move on. Besides, what alternative did she have?

Half an hour later Rosanna stood in the most beautiful bedroom she'd ever seen.

It was airy and spacious and it felt so welcoming. Like a hug embracing her as she entered.

The walls were pale, except for the one behind the canopied bed which was painted with a gorgeous mural of a garden, complete with trellises, fountains, arbours and butterflies flitting between flowers. The furniture looked comfortable and inviting with plenty of plump cushions.

She could imagine herself curled up on that vast divan with the amber-and-gold throw, reading a book or looking out onto the internal courtyard garden. There were beautiful rugs, the sort for which Dhalkur was famous, in shades ranging from cinnamon to amber, dusky rose and dark garnet red.

Along one wall, tall arched windows gave out onto a broad terrace edged with crenellations beyond which, far below, stretched the vast southern plain of Dhalkur and the capital, a blue smudge in the distance.

The scent of roses was everywhere, from the potted

plants on the terrace to the embossed gilt bowls in the room, filled with blooms of every shade.

Through an open doorway she spied a vast, sunken tub in a bathroom that glowed in the early light with shades of amber, gold and mother-of-pearl.

'I've died and gone to heaven,' Rosanna murmured as she stepped inside, her hand automatically reaching for a bowl of perfect roses, some of which, she realised, still held beads of dew. She inhaled, shutting her eyes against a sudden overload of joy.

She'd agreed to a week of sex with Salim. They could have gone to another city, or left the country for an anonymous hotel. Instead he'd brought her somewhere so romantic she had trouble swallowing over the lump rising in her throat.

Over the past four days she'd alternated between exhilaration and a nagging fear that this attraction wasn't as significant for him as it was for her. He'd proven her wrong, bringing her to a place that was clearly special to his family. That showed a level of respect and thoughtfulness that banished her doubts and created an overwhelming surge of emotion.

His thoughtfulness made her feel special. As if she mattered to him.

At the same time she felt more vulnerable than ever. She wrapped her arms around her middle, trying to hold back her swelling emotions.

'I'm glad you like it.'

Salim's voice came from just behind her, making her shiver as his voice hit that rumbling note that never failed to soften her feminine core and scramble her wits.

He stood close. She felt his breath feather her hair and his body heat against her back. Just that was enough to make her breasts feel fuller and damp heat form between her thighs.

Rosanna snapped her eyes open and focused on the beautiful room, rather than the urge to swing around, plaster herself against him and beg for him to take her.

'It's very special. It radiates welcome and wellbeing.'

And Romance with a capital *R*, but she didn't mention that. Because it would be dangerous thinking of Salim and romance together.

This was about lust, she told herself firmly. It was a pragmatic choice to scratch a physical itch and get it out of their systems. She couldn't afford to weave any other fantasies about Salim.

Rosanna blinked, horrified to discover that from joy her emotions had swung abruptly to distress.

'Would you like tea after our journey? Or breakfast? You must be hungry.'

She should be. They'd left so early that she hadn't eaten. Presumably their early start had been to avoid being seen together.

Rosanna pressed a hand to her suddenly churning stomach. She wasn't used to the idea of a secret relationship. As if it, or she, were shameful. 'No thanks, I'm fine.'

Silence. Was it imagination or did her skin tighten as she waited for Salim to speak?

'Perhaps you need to rest. We had a very early start.'

'No!' The word was out before she realised she'd formed it. 'I'm perfectly fine and wide awake.'

Still he didn't touch her. Why?

*Because he's giving you the courtesy of time and space to adjust. Because he's a decent man who won't pounce on you the moment you're alone together.*

Rosanna swallowed, her throat aching with tension. 'There *is* something I want.'

'Yes?'

She felt him move closer, his body mirroring hers, his breath tickling her ear.

'Make love to me, Salim.'

# CHAPTER TEN

IT WAS EXACTLY what he planned to do. Yet Rosanna's words were a cold blast to his overheated libido.

*Make love*, she'd said, and for a second he'd been in total agreement. Till he read the nuance of her words.

He'd brought her here because it was one of his favourite places, plus it was close enough to the city that he could return quickly in an emergency.

He'd given instructions that the place be prepared for them and he'd enjoyed planning to please Rosanna. He'd instructed that the suite be filled with roses because he thought she'd enjoy them, and because they reminded him of her. Her skin was as velvety as any damask petal and as fragrant. She could be thorny too but at heart there was a honeyed sweetness that was irresistible.

Yet, now they were here, he realised how she might misinterpret things. He planned a sybaritic week of sex and relaxation. What he'd given her was a romantic bower.

Worse, though she had no way of knowing, he realised it had never been a place where sheikhs dallied with passing lovers. It had been transformed into a special place by one ruler for the queen he loved. Only queens and their families stayed here.

Yet how could he hold back from Rosanna? He'd already lashed his arm around her waist and hauled her back against him.

He breathed deep, trying to summon restraint. The whole drive here he'd fought a hard-on that had made driving a chore and tested his patience to the limit.

Salim bent his head and used his free hand to drag her hair out of the way so he could nip at her neck. She shuddered in response, her head lolling to one side in invitation.

He loved her eager passion. Rosanna might be a feisty woman and in business matters a formidable negotiator, but when it came to intimacy her instant responsiveness was everything he could want.

Yet he hesitated to take her to the bed which, he realised now, was strewn with blush-pink petals.

Because this wasn't the beginning of some sweet romance that would end with a happy ever after. He didn't want her misinterpreting.

He needed to dispel that fantasy, though he had no intention of giving up Rosanna and all the pleasure they would share over the next week. On the contrary, he intended to use them both to the limit and squeeze every possible erotic pleasure from the time they had. Because he already knew a week would barely be time to take his fill of this remarkable woman.

She moved, her backside swaying from side to side as if inviting him to take her, and fire shot through his groin.

Salim licked her earlobe then nipped there, harder than before, and she gasped, her hands grabbing his encircling arm. She was as turned on as he.

'Is this what you want?' he whispered against her ear as he shoved his other hand between her legs, cupping her mound hard through her jeans.

'Yes.' Her response was a raw groan that lifted the hairs at his nape and made his jeans grow uncomfortable.

A taut smile dragged at his facial muscles as he widened his stance to take her weight a little more. In the process he caught sight of their reflection in the mirrored wall of the bathroom through the open doorway and his pulse stopped. He saw Rosanna, head back against his chest, eyes closed in an expression of bliss, gasping in pleasure as he rubbed his hand between her legs.

'More. Please, Salim.'

'As you wish, my rose.'

Still keeping one arm wrapped around her middle, he flicked open the button of her jeans, then dragged down the zip. He tugged at the denim and it slid down but snagged on her hips. 'Help me.'

She lifted her hands from his arm and shoved her jeans down.

'Now the rest,' he murmured, inserting a finger through the side elastic of her underwear. She grabbed the other side and together they slid the lacy triangle down.

Salim's chest tightened around his snared breath. She still wore her plain white shirt, not some diaphanous lingerie. Yet the sight of her bare, sweetly curving hips and that glossy dark swatch of pubic hair cupped between her slender legs was one of the most arousing sights he'd beheld.

He swallowed, fighting the impulse to rip his own jeans off and power into her without any preliminaries. He owed her more than that.

Her eyes fluttered open and he caught a dazed silvery gleam as she frowned and made to turn towards him. 'Salim?'

'No. Stay like that.'

He cupped her again, this time with no constraining fabric between them and felt her feminine heat, the tickle of soft hair and a dampness that made him smile. Rosanna shuddered, her eyes drifting shut as he slid his hand lower, curving back between her now open thighs. She shifted against him, allowing him access, and once again gripped his supporting arm with both hands.

'Easy, sweetheart.'

Though even as he said it he realised there was no need to wait. No reason at all. Hard and fast would be some consolation after the tortured loneliness of his empty bed. And it might help dispel any misunderstanding about this being a romantic tryst.

Salim pulled her closer so Rosanna leaned back against him as he slipped his hand again between her legs, into that cleft where he found her sensitive bud. She jolted and pressed against him as he slid into her wetness, probing gently.

Rosanna's hips moved in a telltale twist of need as his fingers slid further, deeper.

'You like that, Rosanna?' he whispered in her ear.

He could tell from every movement of her body, and by her desperate expression in the mirror, that she was close. Maybe she'd been as aroused as he on the trip here, anticipating the moment when they came together again.

She might have read his mind. 'Yes. But I want more.'

This time, instead of leaning into his hand she tilted her pelvis back, grinding her buttocks against him, drawing all the blood in his body to his rock-hard erection.

It would be the work of a moment to strip free of his jeans and plunge into her. Except he wanted more too. He wanted her absolutely frantic for him.

So Salim gritted his jaw and dragged the arm at her waist higher so he could cup one luscious breast while sliding his other hand along the slick track of delight between her soft thighs.

Her legs trembled. Her breathing turned to a series of gasps as her head lolled back against him. Salim read the signs of approaching orgasm. Her jerky movements, the rush of moisture against his hand, the musky perfume of female arousal. He bit down at the base of her neck where she was so sensitive.

Rosanna's whole body shuddered. He felt her convulsions from his buried fingertips right down to the soles of his feet as she fell into ecstasy, calling his name. He'd never heard anything so heartfelt, so mesmerising.

And through it all he watched her in the mirror and felt something stronger than satisfaction. It felt much darker than gratification that he'd given a lover pleasure. It felt like possessiveness.

Which was nonsense. It was just a masculine response to the delicious sight of Rosanna in the throes of bliss.

Yet he battled the feeling that this was more than simple sex. She captivated him.

It was just that the wait to claim his lover again had been too long. He wasn't used to waiting for any woman. His liaisons in the past had been much less complicated. The illusion would pass once he'd reached his own climax.

Rosanna was still shaking when he slipped his hand into his back pocket and drew out a condom.

'Here, lean against this.'

His voice was guttural with repressed need as he gently moved Rosanna sideways so she could grasp the back of a high sofa. As soon as he knew she could support herself he undid his jeans and sheathed himself. Even that practised movement was fraught with danger. He was so aroused he feared he mightn't last.

So instead of lifting Rosanna over onto the sofa, he moved behind her, bending his knees and positioning himself at the centre of her feminine heat.

Any fear that she'd had enough after that orgasm faded as she shimmied her hips, drawing up higher to accommodate him more easily. There, he nudged her entrance and lightning jagged through him.

'Ready?'

For answer she pushed her rump towards him, enclosing him in damp heat.

That was it. Salim couldn't wait. He grabbed her hips and thrust long and true, on and on, right to her heart.

The sensation of her tight, wet heat folding around him like a closing fist sent a tremor of raw excitement down his spine and through his groin.

'Yes,' he hissed, barely able to hear the word over the pounding in his ears. She felt so good he had to wait, gather his control, before moving again.

But Rosanna was moving. He opened his eyes and saw her wrenching open her shirt buttons, then struggling free of the fabric. She leaned forward enough to slip a hand between them and flick her bra undone. A second later it was gone too and in the mirror he saw her pink-crested breasts bob free.

Salim swallowed a groan. He wasn't going to last long enough to enjoy this as he wanted.

Then she grabbed one of his hands, tugging it free of her hip, and dragged it up her body, planting it with a breathless sigh on her breast.

Yes, that was better. So much better that Salim's thighs were rock hard with the effort not to buck harder.

'Look in the bathroom, Rosanna.'

His voice was so thick it took her a moment to understand. When she did, their eyes met in the mirror, hers widening at the erotic sight they made. Yet she wasn't dismayed. Salim felt the pulse of pleasure through her body.

That was enough to crack his control. He moved, withdrawing so slowly it was exquisite pain, then pushed up hard, into her sweet depths, his hand tight on her breast, his gaze holding hers.

He heard her snatched hiss of breath. Or was that his? He saw her eyes grow hooded with pleasure as she bucked her hips back against him, lodging him deeper still.

She looked so beautiful with her hair loose around her bare shoulders, her skin flushed and mouth panting with every quick breath. Salim slid his other hand from her hip, watching in the mirror as his hair-darkened arm contrasted with her pale skin, and he took the precious weight of her other breast too.

A voice inside cried out in triumph and he moved again, this time not pausing, simply following the dictates of his animal brain that pushed him higher and deeper, stronger and harder.

But most profound of all was the sense of shared purpose. The diamond-bright glitter in Rosanna's eyes as she met him thrust for thrust. The arch of her body, the way she pushed her breasts into his hands and quivered when he hit that sweet spot deep inside.

He liked that so much his attention turned from his own needs to finding that spot again and again till, like a desert storm appearing out of nowhere, she convulsed around him.

He had an instant's satisfaction that he'd brought her to another pinnacle, then the storm smashed in and tore him free of the mundane world. Salim hung on, pumping frantically in ecstasy, teetering on that knife edge of need so exquisite it veered towards pain. Then, with a roar of shocked completion, he slumped over her, gathering her to him and burying his face in her scented hair.

Rosanna woke, smiling, to a feeling of warmth and luxurious wellbeing that had become familiar over the past few days.

Salim lay entangled with her, his powerful body encompassing her in the way she adored. He was fast asleep, which wasn't surprising given how little rest they'd had. And how very active he'd been a short time before.

Her smile widened into a grin. She could count on the fingers of one hand the hours Salim had spent away from her since they'd arrived. Then it had only been because even on holiday a sheikh needed to maintain contact with his staff in case anything vital cropped up.

The rest of the time he'd devoted to her.

Sex with Salim had been an eye-opener. Not only did it cast Rosanna's experience with Phil into the shadows, but Salim had made her aware of her sensuality in a way she never had been before.

The morning they'd arrived here was the first time

she'd had sex outside a bed. With Phil they'd always been horizontal, in the dark, usually after a long day at work.

But tiredness alone didn't explain the difference. Salim worked long hours too, and he was definitely not getting enough sleep. Yet he was sexually vigorous and demanding, passionate and adventurous. She revelled in it. Not once had he pushed her to do something she didn't want. In fact, she'd revelled in the freedom to follow her needs fully, making her own demands.

Rosanna shivered, thinking of all the ways they'd enjoyed each other these last few days.

Behind her Salim stirred but didn't wake. Yet even that tiny movement made her hyper-aware of him, his chest against her back, one hairy thigh between her knees and his hand lax on the nest of curls at the apex of her thighs. As if, even in sleep, he claimed her.

She adored the way he never tired of touching her. Often with bold, sexual intent, but not always. How often had he swept her hair from her face then tangled his fingers there, as if fascinated by its softness? Or reached out to brush her cheek or hand in a passing caress?

He took her hand often, especially when they left the palace to explore the surprisingly fertile if rugged landscape.

This morning he'd led her up a narrow mountain path to watch the sun rise. They hadn't gone far but it had felt like another world with the spectacular plain spread before them, gilded by the light.

He'd taken her to a ravine where cyclamens and lilies grew wild and a carpet of other flowers she didn't know. She'd been lost in wonder at the sight of such natural beauty.

Then, still holding her hand, he'd led her to a natural spring, its water bubbling from a cleft in the rock to tumble into a deep pool high above the valley.

Inevitably Salim had persuaded her to join him naked, in the cold water, and they'd made love there, looking out over his land as the sun lifted. The place and the moment had felt magical. Rosanna knew the memory of it, and of how it felt to be cherished by Salim, would last the rest of her life.

That's how she felt. Cherished.

Salim showed her in so many small ways, each day, that she mattered.

Like when he personally brewed tea for her each morning, after learning it was her favourite and that she only drank coffee once she was well into the day. The way he shortened his stride to match hers as they walked together. How he was so solicitous, always offering her choices, like whether she wanted to swim in the palace's mosaic-lined pool, or to go out exploring in the four-wheel drive. Or have sex. He respected her need for rest and never expected her simply to accept what he wanted to do.

They might be having a short, steamy affair. They might spend most of their time naked and sometimes her legs were so weak from prolonged bliss that Salim had to carry her to the sunken tub and stay, in the warm, scented water, to carry her out again. But never had Rosanna felt cheapened or taken for granted.

Salim wasn't that sort of man. She wouldn't be here if he were. That was one good thing to come out of past trauma. She wasn't a woman who'd let herself be taken for granted ever again. They were equals here, no matter what differences society placed on them.

It was heady and wonderful. Salim made her feel

strong and special, as if their lovemaking forged a new power in her. A new confidence that she'd lost somewhere in the last couple of years.

Sexually, he might hold her in thrall but that didn't make her weak. Because she'd seen evidence, time and again, that she had the same effect on him. She mightn't have his experience but Salim needed her as desperately as she needed him. That showed no sign of abating.

Rosanna frowned. This was their fourth day together yet if anything she felt bound more closely to Salim than before. There was no fracture in the ties between them, certainly no boredom or lack of interest.

'Are you all right, my rose?'

Salim's voice was husky with sleep and, she guessed, arousal, since she felt his erection stiffen behind her.

Instantly that frisson of not-quite-anxiety disintegrated, replaced by a familiar coil of anticipation deep inside.

She revelled in that pet name he used so often. As if he saw her as delicate and precious, something she'd never imagined herself to be. It fitted the romantic ambience of this wonderful place, so special with its rich silks and decadent luxuries, its bountiful walled garden and exquisite frescoes. It made her feel as if she belonged here, though she knew that could never be.

'Of course I am. I was just thinking of getting up and leaving you to rest.'

'Alone?' No mistaking his disappointment. Or his intent as he dipped his hand into the downy curls between her legs and found her already damp with wanting. 'Ah, Rosanna.' His voice burred across her skin like the rub of roughened velvet. 'You do like to tease me, don't you?'

Salim shifted, his proud erection solid against her

buttocks, and Rosanna found herself arching back, pressing against all that exciting hardness while his fingers delved deeper and her breath caught.

'You need your sleep,' she gasped, even as her eyes rolled back in sheer bliss. She loved being wanted by this man. She loved that he insisted on pleasing her, every time, often several times, before his own release.

'I was dreaming of you. And no wonder.' His questing fingers made her gasp as delight shimmered through her. 'You can't ask me to go back to sleep now.'

Yet he moved away, all that lovely warmth gone in a second, and Rosanna opened her mouth to protest. Except gentle hands pulled her onto her back and he was above her, the excitement in his eyes contrasting with his almost sombre expression. As if suddenly this wasn't a matter of teasing but something much more serious.

Her feverish buzz stilled as she sensed a change in him. 'Salim?'

Rosanna reached up, wondering at that sober look. Her hands skimmed his chest and shoulders but before she could embrace him, he sank low, settling further down her body. He wrapped his arms around her thighs, pulling them up over his shoulders, and she couldn't stifle another gasp as his hot breath tickled her damp curls.

'Salim, I…'

She lost whatever she'd been about to say as he kissed her intimately and once again made the world fall away.

Salim looked across to Rosanna lying on a padded sun lounger. She was naked but for the diaphanous red caftan she'd insisted on throwing on after their swim. His gaze traced the lines and entrancing curves of her body enticingly revealed through the sheer fabric. He couldn't imagine ever wanting to be anywhere else.

For the first time it occurred to him to wonder what it would be like if he hadn't been born royal, with a nation's expectations on his shoulders, and could please himself with what he did and who he chose to be with.

Hurriedly he thrust away the thought. That could never be.

'Tell me about this place, Salim. It's obviously very old but it has such a warm feel to it. Not grim like a fortress.'

Rosanna's voice was soft and her eyes closed as she lay on her stomach, her cheek pillowed on her folded arms. Even this late in the day it was warm enough for her to settle in the shade rather than bake in the direct sunlight at the edge of the long pool.

'What do you want to know?'

She looked like she wasn't far off sleep and he couldn't blame her. They'd had a vigorous, wholly satisfying afternoon.

He couldn't remember ever feeling so good, fizzing with energy, despite the weighted laxness of his well-used body. Rosanna tested him to the limit, urging him to peak after peak when common sense decreed he should be sated.

A dull clamour of warning sounded in his brain. Like a cracked bell ringing off-key in paradise. He felt the discordant jangle too in the hollowing of his belly.

Salim frowned, trying to identify it. He'd experienced it earlier in bed. He'd rolled her over and looked down into eyes as bright and beguiling as moonlight and felt...

That was it. The temptation to feel too much, read too much into their compatibility, though he knew they'd soon go their separate ways.

Salim ignored the pain stabbing his rib cage. That,

he assured himself, was for Rosanna. He worried about her. He'd seen her dreamy expression as she watched him and feared maybe she was building unrealistic hopes about them.

Yet whenever they talked about the future, Rosanna was as sensible as she'd always been. Expecting nothing from him but this single week.

*He* wanted more than a week. Seven days wouldn't be enough to sever the bond between them.

But it had to be. He'd already gone beyond the limits of what was reasonable.

'Tell me about the queen it was made for,' she said sleepily, and he was reminded irresistibly of himself, years ago, begging his mother for another bedtime story. Time alone with her had been such a treat.

'It wasn't built for a queen but as a clan fortress centuries ago.' His lips quirked up in a smile. 'Times have changed. These days local power struggles are confined to politics.'

Rosanna opened her eyes and surveyed him. He read the dark pewter colour, so different to the bright blaze of silver when she was aroused. This was her assessing look, as if she weighed his words. He knew she was still thinking of the queen, not old power struggles.

Salim shrugged and relented. What harm would it do to tell her? 'It came to the crown when one of our country's greatest sheikhs married the daughter of the clan chieftain of this region. She brought the fortress as part of her dowry.'

'It must have been a powerful clan to give up such a strategic position.'

He nodded, surprised at how quickly she'd grasped its significance. 'It was. Winning her as a bride was a political coup for the sheikh. The irony is that she refused him, not once but twice.'

Rosanna's eyes widened. 'I've heard about her!'

She pushed herself up on her elbows, inadvertently giving Salim a glorious view of her breasts.

A clenching weight in his groin banished that phantom sensation that something was amiss. His palms itched with the need to cup those lovely breasts and caress her till she purred with pleasure. She was so beautiful.

Yet he'd known more classically beautiful women. There was something about Rosanna that he couldn't explain but *felt* at a visceral level.

'The sheikh made those three wonderful gates to the palace to celebrate when she finally agreed to marry him.'

Salim looked into Rosanna's face and knew she'd fallen for the old tale.

Slowly he nodded. 'So the story goes.'

'You don't believe it?' She studied him intently then shrugged, her mouth turning down at the corners, and lay down again.

Instantly Salim regretted puncturing her fantasy. Not because he couldn't see her breasts any more. The view of her back, buttocks and legs was one of the finest vistas he'd ever enjoyed. But because he'd erased that smile.

'I'm not a romantic. But you're right, that's the story. In fact, the story goes that sheikh after sheikh since then married for love.'

Until recently.

Her smile was back, mischievous this time, and he liked that too.

'I love it! All those fierce rulers, so autocratic and powerful, turning weak at the knees for just the right woman.'

Of course she did. It was the sort of fantasy women
adored.

'After he acquired the fortress, the sheikh set about
turning it into a private retreat for himself and his wife,
and eventually their family. Tradition has it that he was
the one who ordered the courtyard to be planted with
flowers as well as the usual fruit trees and medicinal
herbs. In every generation since, changes have been
made, introducing more luxuries. Now the only real
evidence of the fortress are its thick walls and the crenellations along the top.'

'I like the fact it's become a retreat for the royal family. It must be special to you.'

Salim nodded. 'It is. I've been coming here for as
long as I can remember.'

The caretakers here were like family to him, though
on this visit he'd barely seen them, spending all his time
with Rosanna.

'So,' Rosanna mused. 'You come from a long line of
romantics. I find that hard to believe.'

She didn't need to mention his businesslike search
for a wife. It was there between them, the elephant in
the room. Time enough for that when they returned to
the city.

'You're right. But I'm not actually descended from
them.'

'You're not?' Her eyes snapped open. 'I thought the
title passed from father to son?'

'It does. Usually to the elder son, though in my case
the Royal Council chose me over Fuad.'

An action which had sent his brother storming from
the capital in a fit of fury. Straight to his death in a man-

gle of metal when his too-powerful car had crashed on a road not built for Formula One–style racing.

What would have happened if Fuad had survived? Salim couldn't imagine him quietly sitting on the sidelines while his younger brother ruled.

'How is it that you're not from the same line?'

Salim hauled his thoughts back from Fuad's death and his own conflicted feelings. He'd have done anything to save his brother, but he had no illusions about his character. There'd never been anything like love between them.

'Two generations ago the sheikh had only one child, a daughter. But under our constitution a woman can't inherit the Dhalkuri throne. His wife died and he was urged year after year to take a new wife to get a male heir and secure the succession.'

He paused, checking to see that Rosanna understood, which she clearly did, given her attentiveness.

'The sheikh refused because he'd loved his wife and didn't want to replace her. Eventually he relented when he realised how worried his people were about instability if he had no clear successor. So he married the respected widow of his best friend. A woman who already had one son. He adopted the boy as his legal heir and that boy grew up to be my father.'

'That's so romantic, that the old sheikh didn't want to marry after he lost his first wife.'

Salim nodded. Seeing that dreamy look in her eyes he didn't add the story he'd heard privately, that the old sheikh's second marriage hadn't been consummated because he couldn't bear to sleep with a woman other than his first wife. That would only cement Rosanna's romantic imaginings.

'What happened to his daughter? The one who couldn't inherit?'

'She married. They're both dead now but their daughter, Tara, my cousin, is still in the region. She married the Sheikh of Nahrat, across the border. I saw her recently and she's very happy.'

He was glad for her. He'd always liked Tara and it was good to see her thriving.

Salim looked at Rosanna's tender smile and the glow in her eyes. It was a shame but he couldn't let her weave romantic imaginings. It was too dangerous.

'I missed the romantic tradition. My parents' marriage was an arranged one. My mother was a princess from a nearby kingdom and brought a lot of valuable resources with her. Fuad and I were raised to expect something similar. To choose brides who would benefit our nation, not someone we fell for.'

'You don't believe in love?'

Her tone wasn't wistful. In fact, he couldn't catch any inflection there, yet Salim sensed there was more to her question than simple curiosity.

Which wouldn't do. It was too dangerous.

He lifted his shoulders in a shrug. 'I believe romantic love exists because there are people who swear they've experienced it.'

Actually, watching his cousin, Tara, Salim *knew* it existed. She and Raif were head over heels in love. But she came from a different background.

'No one in my immediate biological family has experienced it. Not me or my brother. Not my parents or my parents' parents. I suspect susceptibility to love might be something you inherit or acquire from your family.

But in my family…' He paused and shook his head emphatically, watching Rosanna closely to be sure she got the message. 'No. Definitely not.'

# CHAPTER ELEVEN

ROSANNA LOOKED UP from the book she was trying to read and shut it with a sigh.

She couldn't concentrate. Salim's revelations about this place and his family kept circling in her head.

The tale of a long-ago king, consumed with love for his proud bride who wasn't easily won. The romantic in Rosanna responded to the idea of him planning a dynastic marriage and instead succumbing to love. And all his descendants too. She didn't know much Dhalkuri history but even she had heard that its leaders were famed as fierce and indomitable.

Yet it wasn't the long-ago past that occupied her thoughts. It was Salim. The sharp, assessing look he'd given her when he carefully explained he was *not* descended from the same stock. That his family didn't marry for love.

Rosanna understood.

It was a reminder that Salim would marry sensibly. He'd choose a partner who met his exacting criteria, to satisfy him and the needs of his country. There was no question of him falling in love.

No question of him falling for *her*.

Which was a good thing.

Neither of them wanted that sort of complication.

After Phil she wasn't ready for a long-term relationship. The thought of falling in love scared her. It would take a lot for her to give her trust to another man.

Plus she didn't need Salim to warn her of all the reasons why she wouldn't make a suitable match for him. She spoke only English and a few phrases of schoolgirl German. She had no diplomatic experience. She didn't feel at home mixing with royalty or national leaders. As for being tall, blonde and free from scandal in her past...

Rosanna shifted abruptly and the book slid from her lap to the ruby-coloured cushions of the window seat where she was curled up. She reached out and pulled the carved wooden screen further open so she had a clear view across to the next mountain peak.

The sun was setting, bathing the world in an apricot glow. Light caught the spray from a tiny mountain stream, creating a hazy rainbow that turned the nearby ravine into a magical place.

A weight pressed down on her lungs.

She didn't believe in magic.

Since Phil she barely believed in romance, despite her fondness for stories with happy endings. Which was why she'd been able to accept Salim's proposition. It was the only way forward. The only way to survive her all-encompassing fascination with this man.

She had to believe that by sating this hunger she could conquer it and move on. Having this honest relationship, where she and Salim shared the truth unvarnished by the trappings of romance, made her stronger. She was taking control of her pleasure and her life choices.

When it was over she could return to getting her life back on track after the disaster she'd left behind in

Australia. She could focus on her career and eventually, maybe one day when her soul had healed, she'd meet a man she could trust and care for.

It all made eminent sense. Why then had she felt hurt when Salim excused himself to visit the family of caretakers here? He'd explained that he'd known them since childhood and it would be rude not to see them.

Rosanna had watched him leave for the house tucked into the walls on the outside of the palace and felt... desolate.

Didn't he believe her good enough to meet his friends? Was he ashamed of her?

Rosanna's fingers tightened on the intricate carving. The screen was beautiful and provided a filter for the sunlight. Yet it was a reminder of a time when women lived restricted lives. Such screens had sometimes been a barrier between them and the outside world.

It was fanciful but suddenly Rosanna felt isolated and lonely. Not because of the palace's secluded location, which actually appealed, but because Salim chose not to take her with him.

She frowned. She was used to looking after herself, holding down taxing jobs and keeping busy. She was happy in her own company. Yet none of that mattered against the fact Salim chose not to introduce her into this tiny fraction of his personal life.

She was good enough for an affair but not to meet his friends.

Rosanna's mouth flattened. She couldn't even be angry because Salim was right. It wasn't that he was ashamed of her but that he was avoiding unnecessary complications. Introducing her to his friends would raise expectations and the need for explanations in the future.

He was saving both of them discomfort.

Yet it didn't sit well with her.

Even so, it was a timely reminder of why they'd come here. And what would happen when they left.

Nothing. Nothing but the conclusion of her work then her return to London to more work for Marian.

She had to focus on that. And getting Salim out of her system as soon as possible. Because the alternative, of this affair not curing her need for him, was too frightening to consider.


'Are you sure you feel up to a hike this morning?'

Normally Salim welcomed any opportunity to get outdoors, especially here where he had the luxury of almost guaranteed solitude. But Rosanna must be exhausted this morning. He felt the delicious lassitude that came after great sex. He wouldn't mind basking in bed then having a late breakfast with her, and then starting all over again.

'Of course. I'm looking forward to that view of the mountain villages you promised.' She paused in the act of getting out of bed and slanted a look over her shoulder before her gaze slid away. 'Unless you'd rather not.'

Rosanna's voice didn't sound right.

She sounded diffident.

Surely not. Not after the way they'd spent the last hour, sharing incredible intimacies and a level of bliss that astounded him. Diffidence was the last thing he expected from Rosanna. She was competent, assured, sexy and eager to make the most of this week. This woman wasn't meek or shy.

He thought of how she'd greeted him on his return yesterday afternoon. He'd felt uncomfortable, almost guilty, returning from the warm embrace of his friends and feeling that he should have invited Rosanna to join him.

Not that she'd pushed for that. But her curiosity about his country and its traditions, plus the fact she was a guest alone in his country with little opportunity to make acquaintances, had weighed heavily on him. It had been selfish not to invite her. Because, he realised, she was *his* secret and, like a miser hoarding gold, he didn't want to share her with anyone.

Maybe too he'd needed some distance because with Rosanna he'd felt unsettling emotions stir.

He'd returned, half expecting to find her brooding or sulky, maybe a little cool with him.

Instead she'd sauntered up to him with a provocative sway to her hips and a hooded, sensual look in her eyes, and invited him to join her for a naked dip. The fact she'd worn nothing but that gauzy scarlet caftan had decided the matter.

Guilt had receded, replaced by instant lust. They'd spent the rest of the evening teasing and pleasing each other. Rosanna's single-minded focus on exploring their mutual passion had brought him undone several times. It was a miracle either of them had the energy to slide out of bed this morning.

Yet there she was, on her feet by the bed, a question in her eyes.

'Of course I—' he began.

'We needn't go as far as the villages—'

They both stopped. She thought he was afraid she'd insist on visiting a mountain village?

A bitter tang filled his mouth as he realised she thought he didn't want to be seen with her. His chest tightened. Did she think he was ashamed of her?

'We can go as far as you like,' he offered. 'I thought you might be tired.'

As he was. Not that it stopped him greedily devouring the sight of her nakedness. He'd never tire of her body. Even clothed she had a grace that caught at something high in his throat, and, he admitted, deep in his groin.

She shrugged one shoulder, making Salim marvel at how she could turn a casual gesture into something that made his whole being clench with desire. Not just physical desire either, but something more puzzling.

The desire to keep her with him. As his.

Shock slammed into him, jerking his head back. Something cleaved through his gut. Warning? Or fear?

He was imagining things. He was just feeling the aftereffects of hours of erotic play. A connection that seemed profound because of its intensity. But soon it would begin waning.

'Okay then, I'll have a quick shower and dress. I'd like to get out into the countryside.' She paused. 'But I'll understand if you change your mind. I could always go for a stroll by myself.'

There it was again, that hint of diffidence. It didn't sit well with the indomitable, fascinating woman he knew.

Before Salim could answer she walked quickly to the bathroom. To forestall further discussion?

He opened his mouth to stop her then closed it. What would he say? Apologise for leaving her yesterday? But it had been the sensible thing to do, protecting her privacy and avoiding speculation.

Yet he found his jaw was clenched and his belly cramped. He didn't like leaving the conversation that way, feeling he'd done wrong by her.

Salim forked his fingers through his hair, unaccustomed to this indecisiveness.

But one decision was obvious. No matter how much he wanted to make amends and see Rosanna's glorious smile, he would *not* follow her into the shower. It would scupper anything like clear thought for a long time to come.

Salim needed all his wits about him.

What had begun as a simple solution to inconvenient lust felt far more complex than he'd anticipated.

An hour later, after breakfast at Rosanna's favourite spot on the terrace, they were ready to set out. Rosanna was bright and seemingly full of energy.

Too much energy? Was her good cheer a little brittle?

Salim shook his head, annoyed at his imaginings, and led the way around the building and past the empty stables. Next time he visited he'd ensure the stables were restocked. The area was perfect for riding and Salim missed it.

He imagined riding with Rosanna through the mountains to some of his favourite places. Until he remembered they wouldn't come here together again.

'Your Majesty.'

Salim paused as a tall, familiar figure emerged from the last stable door.

'Murad! It's good to see you.'

The older man bent deep in a gesture of obeisance, reminding Salim abruptly of all that had passed since they'd last met.

'Please rise.'

In other circumstances he would have embraced the old man, but Murad would feel uncomfortable since they weren't alone. Salim had seen his gaze flick to Rosanna.

'My sympathies on your loss, Your Majesty. Your father was a good man and an excellent ruler.'

'Thank you, Murad. He was indeed. I hope to fulfil his expectations of me.'

'You will, Majesty. That's certain.' He smiled and Salim couldn't hold back any longer. He grasped the old man's hand in both his.

'I feel better for seeing you, my old friend.' He turned to Rosanna. 'This is Murad Darwish. He used to be caretaker at the Queen's Palace until he retired a few years ago. I've known him all my life.'

He was like a de facto grandfather.

'Murad, I'd like you to meet Ms Rosanna MacIain, who's visiting from London.'

He watched with pleasure as the two shook hands, and Rosanna surprised him by greeting his friend in his own language then observing in the same language that it was a fine day. Naturally Murad was delighted.

'You came to visit your family?' Salim asked, continuing to speak English. He didn't want Rosanna feeling excluded.

Murad's son and daughter-in-law were now the palace caretakers while Murad lived in his village several kilometres away.

'I'll see them, but I came to see you, Your Majesty.' He gestured to the open door beside them. 'If you will.'

Knowing it was useless to protest the formal title, Salim entered the stables.

'Oh, how gorgeous!'

Rosanna saw the puppies at the same time he did. Murad opened the stall and she hurried forward as a tumbling bundle of fur resolved itself into a couple of puppies. They already showed fair to mature into the elegant, long-legged hunting dogs so familiar to him. At the moment their plumed tails seemed out of proportion, like their oversized paws.

Memory hit Salim. Of the pedigreed dogs who'd always lived at the royal palaces. They'd been his father's pride and joy. To Salim, who'd spent hours in the kennels and stables, they'd been playmates. His chest tightened as he recalled being abroad when Fuad cleared both stables and kennels in their father's last days.

'They're fine-looking animals.' He bent to stroke one silky ear then watched indulgently as the pup wriggled enthusiastically and tried to nip his fingers.

'Bred from your father's finest stock.'

'Really? You managed to save them?'

'Some.' Murad shook his head sadly. 'Some trusted people helped rescue others.'

Rosanna looked up from where she squatted, playing with a pup.

'Thank you, Murad. I appreciate it.'

Murad inclined his head. 'Since they're from the royal kennels I wanted to present one to you. That's why I'm here, with the two finest pups of the litter.'

Strangely, Salim felt his throat tighten. The gift was generous when a dog with such a pedigree would fetch a lot of money. More, it was the reminder of his dead father and of times gone by that hit him. And recognition of Murad's role in his own life as mentor and friend.

'Thank you, Murad. That's a generous gift indeed.'

'I'm pleased you think so.' Murad paused. 'If you permit I'll let my family know I've arrived while you make your choice.'

The old man might have been a diplomat, for he'd surely guessed at Salim's sudden upsurge of emotions, though Salim was sure his expression had revealed nothing. He'd been taught to conceal his emotions as befitted a prince. But the old man knew him better than most. He knew how much he admired his father, despite the formality that had existed between them.

Salim hunkered down and was immediately mobbed by two eager puppies. He grinned, his hands sinking deep into soft fur.

'You're a dog person.'

He shrugged. 'We always had dogs and horses in the palace.' He looked up to see Rosanna's keen-eyed stare fixed on him. 'So are you. You're a natural with them.'

'With four children in the family there were always pets at home. Always at least one dog and a couple of rabbits. There was a blue tongue lizard too at one stage and several mice.'

Salim like the sound of it, informal and fun. 'It sounds like quite a menagerie.'

'Says the man who grew up with kennels and stables.'

Her generous smile conveyed only humour, not jealousy.

That set her apart from many. Often people's view of him was tinged by his privileged upbringing. It was true he'd never lacked for food, shelter or money. Yet the demands of royal life and expectations meant he'd missed out on the more informal joys of normal family life. Not that he was complaining. It was just a difference between him and others. Yet Rosanna teased him as easily as if there were no gulf between them. He liked that.

'Did you have a dog of your own?'

The question dimmed his burgeoning smile. 'For a short time.'

It had been a pup like these, with bright eyes and feet too big for its body. Salim had adored it.

'I'm sorry. Not a good memory?'

Salim shrugged as a pup, the one with the remarkable black colouring so rare in its breed, licked his hand. The raspy caress unlocked something inside him he'd almost forgotten. Or maybe it was Rosanna's silence. He knew she was curious but she didn't push for details. Whatever the reason, suddenly he wanted to share.

What could it hurt? He owed precious little loyalty to Fuad. Plus he knew Rosanna would never tell anyone. Salim settled more comfortably, his back against the stall wall.

'I was given a pup for my fifth birthday. I loved dogs and my parents thought it would be a good way to learn responsibility. Unfortunately that made my elder brother jealous. He'd never been given a dog.'

He saw Rosanna frown. He knew it sounded like favouritism, and Fuad used to accuse him of being their mother's favourite because she'd sometimes sit with him when he had nightmares. 'He hated dogs so it would have been pointless giving him one as a pet.'

'That's sad. Had he been bitten by one?'

'Not that I know of.' Salim scratched the belly of the pup now lying on its back before him. 'He didn't like animals of any sort and they didn't like him.'

Salim remembered horses shying when Fuad approached and dogs barking aggressively or cringing away. As if they sensed the cruel streak that he seldom bothered to hide when he was alone with his little brother.

'My dog went missing and was eventually found at the bottom of an old well in the courtyard.' He met Rosanna's stare. 'No one could understand how he fell in when there was wire mesh over the top. Until a sta-blehand came forward to say he'd seen Fuad drop the dog in.'

'Oh, Salim!' Her eyes rounded and she leaned for-ward, grabbing his hand with hers. She looked aghast. 'That's horrible! Was it true?'

'Fuad denied it but he was never allowed alone in the kennels or stables after that. Not that he minded.'

But their father had found other punishments for him. Fuad had blamed Salim for that, taking out his anger on his younger brother whenever he could, know-ing Salim wouldn't run crying to their parents. Even as a child Salim had had more pride and foolhardy obsti-nacy than to admit weakness before his brother.

'I'm so sorry.' Her remarkable eyes glittered in sympathy. 'It must have been tough growing up with a brother like that.'

'We weren't close,' he said eventually.

But Rosanna wasn't finished. He should have re-alised she'd guess. 'You said your father's dogs needed saving. Because of your brother?'

He looked at her, sitting cross-legged with a now sleepy dog in her lap. Its pale grey pelt reminded him of the prize hounds of which his father had been so proud. Anger stirred at Fuad's petty vengefulness.

Finally he nodded. 'When our father's terminal ill-ness worsened Fuad assumed control, acting on his behalf. I was abroad getting investors for some devel-opment schemes in Dhalkur and didn't realise how ill my father had become. Neither he nor Fuad mentioned it whenever I rang home.'

Salim still felt guilty over that.

'And something happened while you were away.'

He released a slow breath. 'Fuad ordered the stables and kennels emptied. The horses were sold but the dogs… He gave instructions that they simply be got rid of.'

'You mean killed?'

Salim nodded. 'I knew most of them somehow escaped but not what happened to them.'

Her fingers squeezed his. 'Your friend Murad is a good man. No wonder you like him so much.'

'I'm lucky to have him in my life.'

Salim paused, thinking of how he'd resisted the urge to quiz Rosanna about *her* past, trying to keep some distance in their relationship.

Distance! What a laugh. He felt closer to Rosanna than to anyone he knew.

That realisation rocked him.

He had friends and people he'd known all his life, but no one close enough to talk with like this.

'Salim? What is it?'

'Nothing important. Tell me more about the menagerie at home and all your siblings. Are you still close?'

It turned out they were and Rosanna didn't mind talking about her family in the least. She described her three brothers and her childhood in suburban Sydney. She spoke of backyard games and netball competitions. Of swimming lessons and holidays on the coast. Of her beloved border collie who'd finally died just as she left home for university.

Salim sat, relaxed, stroking the dog beside him, and felt transported to a world that felt exotic and appealing. Because of the warmth and charm Rosanna exuded as she reminisced. He wanted to see the old apple tree where they'd built a treehouse and taste her mother's best ever roast and apple crumble. Hear more about the compassion and common-sense values instilled by her social worker father and school librarian mother.

It was a far cry from his own upbringing.

'And the man you planned to marry? What about him?'

As soon as he said it, Salim realised he'd destroyed the relaxed mood. Rosanna stiffened, her hand poised in mid-stroke over the dog nestled in her lap.

'Phil? He's no longer in my life.'

'How did you meet?'

'At work. I was employed to recruit senior staff for a major financial institution. He worked there and we hit it off.'

Salim watched her mouth flatten and felt inordinately pleased that there was clearly nothing now between her and her ex-fiancé. Not that it was any of his business.

'You were together long?'

She shrugged. 'Long enough to think of marriage.'

'So you were obviously compatible.'

Rosanna shot him a look from under lowered brows. 'I thought so but I was mistaken.'

It was clear she didn't want to discuss this and Salim should do her the courtesy of stopping. Yet he needed to know more. Because if he wasn't mistaken, that was pain he read in her expression and he didn't like the way that made him feel.

'He hurt you?'

She looked away. 'I trusted him and he betrayed me, so yes, he hurt me.' She turned back, meeting his gaze almost defiantly. 'I'm more wary now. I thought I knew him but I was wrong and that undermined my confidence. But I've adjusted my expectations. I won't make the same mistake again.'

Her lips turned up in a smile that didn't meet her

eyes and she began talking of the dogs, of how hard it would be to choose between them.

Salim listened but with only half an ear. He was far more interested in Rosanna's revelations and what they told him about her.

Her ex had betrayed her. With another woman?

The man had poor taste. How could he want another woman when he had Rosanna?

Salim thought of her professionalism and competence and wondered how she'd coped when her ex undermined her confidence. She never gave any indication that was the case, standing up to Salim and challenging him to be realistic in his requirements. That only strengthened his admiration.

But what made him most curious was her statement that she'd adjusted her expectations. Had she closed off her heart, not believing she could trust a man after that betrayal?

That saddened him. This woman deserved more. She deserved not just honesty but a man who would devote his life to her.

Salim's thoughts turned to what *he'd* offered her. A week's carnal pleasure. A chance to gratify his yearning for her before they returned to the capital and he set her to work finding him a wife.

Suddenly his actions seemed not pragmatic but selfish. Not clear-sighted but crass. Even after their affair ended, to expect her to help him choose a bride...

Distaste churned in his belly at the idea he'd taken advantage of a woman who'd already had her hopes and expectations destroyed by a man.

Salim should have treated her better. Not that Rosanna complained. But the very fact that she'd agreed to his proposition, and that she responded so fully and generously to him, made him feel less than the man he wanted to be.

But what else could he have offered her? It was this short affair or nothing.

And despite what honour urged, *nothing* hadn't been an option. He was a man of strong self-control but even one more day together in his palace and he wouldn't have been able to keep his hands off her.

Salim watched Rosanna smile as she stroked the silvery puppy that he feared would always remind him of her beautiful eyes. He thought of the day, soon, when she'd return to Britain. He'd never see her again unless she attended his wedding to the nameless woman who would hopefully meet his all-important criteria, because his country needed her.

Strange. In the past he'd thought of his bride with the resignation of a busy man who saw her as another job to be ticked off.

Now he actively disliked that faceless woman.

# CHAPTER TWELVE

ROSANNA LAY, PANTING and flushed, across Salim's heaving chest. Their lovemaking had been vigorous and satisfying and something else too. But she refused to analyse why it had felt different. Meaningful. Profound.

No, she wasn't going there!

She'd promised herself not to weave fantasies about Salim. She couldn't afford to begin now.

No matter how tempting.

What did it matter that today in the stables, and later when he'd taken her to a village where they'd been warmly welcomed, she'd felt special? Because Salim had shared so much with her. Because he'd drawn her into his world on yet another, personal, level.

He'd let her glimpse a slice of his private life that she could tell he treasured. She hugged that to herself like the precious gift it was.

Salim had taken her first to the palace caretaker's home where he'd introduced her to Murad's family and pleased the old man by accepting the beautiful black hound as a gift, before purchasing the other pup at a very handsome price.

Then the two men had led her to Murad's village. She'd drunk sweetened tea and eaten almond and honey sweets. She'd exchanged halting pleasantries with the locals and been rewarded with wide smiles. The women had proudly shown her their weaving and the roses they cultivated to sell for their fragrant essence. She'd had fun with the children too. They'd invited her to join in a local version of hopscotch, teaching her to count the numbers in their language and crowing with approval at her success.

Rosanna had left with a smile on her face and a warm glow inside.

'The people here are so friendly,' she murmured against Salim's chest. 'I had a wonderful time today.'

'They love visitors,' he murmured, wrapping his arm around her back. 'Guests are always welcome.'

Rosanna thought about the small but scrupulously clean homes she'd seen. The rough but magnificent terrain that didn't yield easily to the plough yet supported the scattered villages. The sense of community.

'They seem very happy.'

He stroked her hair over her shoulder and she stretched into his touch. He made her feel like purring.

'Dhalkuris are hardy and resilient, and we love our country.' He paused. 'They appreciated that you spoke their language. When did you learn?'

'You make it sound like I'm fluent. I only know greetings and a couple of other words.' Yet Salim's acknowledgement felt like high praise. She'd worked to perfect her few phrases. 'I had free time in the evenings.'

Maybe those lonely nights were part of the reason she'd so fixated on Salim.

'Your assistant, Taqi, helped. I asked him to correct my pronunciation. He's a stickler but it paid off when the villagers understood me.'

She felt proud. Before coming to Dhalkur she'd never

conversed in another language outside a classroom and it felt amazing when she actually communicated. Maybe she'd continue learning when she left here. But instead of pleasing her, the idea flattened her smile. She didn't want to think of leaving.

Just as she didn't like the trill of Salim's phone. She knew that ringtone, knew it meant a call he wouldn't ignore.

Sure enough, Salim excused himself and slid out from beneath her, rolling to the far side of the bed and rising to sit with his back to her as he reached for the phone.

Rosanna lay, drinking in the sight of his powerful frame, his rumpled dark hair and wide, straight shoulders. For now at least he was hers and—

Something about his stillness caught her attention. The way he suddenly sat straighter, raking his hand through his hair in a gesture of impatience or frustration.

Slowly he lowered the phone and put it on the bedside table. He didn't turn immediately but sat as if staring at the view beyond the window. Except the sun had gone and the panorama was in darkness.

A chill crept along Rosanna's bones and her happiness froze into a hard lump, heavy inside her.

'Salim?'

Her voice sounded surprisingly normal. Not as if it emerged from a throat constricting with fear.

Then he swivelled around, his eyes meeting hers, and every unvoiced fear was realised.

Her heart crashed against her ribs as shock ran through her. 'It's bad news, isn't it?'

He shook his head. But in the few minutes since he'd slid out from beneath her, he'd altered. He looked sterner, his gaze shuttered. There was a distance between them far greater than the width of the bed. Salim was back in regal mode and she hated it.

Because she knew what that meant.

'Not bad news. Actually, it's good. There's been an unexpected breakthrough in some international negotiations.'

Rosanna said nothing, waiting for what she knew was coming.

'But it means I'm needed. This final stage of the negotiation will be between heads of state.' He paused and she saw a fleeting expression that looked like regret. 'Either I go to the capital or I bring the negotiations here.'

Which he wouldn't do. This was his private bolthole. Nor would he want to advertise her presence.

'When do you leave?'

For a long moment he didn't answer.

'Now.'

Salim watched her flinch and had to brace himself not to lunge across the bed and gather her close. He wanted to bury his head in her fragrant hair, bury himself in her warm, lush body and forget about the outside world.

He wanted to ignore duty and the peace treaty that had been his priority since taking the throne.

He wanted to curse and throw his phone across the room and stick his head in the sand.

He wanted to stay here.

*He wanted Rosanna.*

That was the problem. He still wanted her as much as he had when they'd arrived. More so. If anything their time together had strengthened their bond.

How could he have fooled himself that this short interlude would satisfy him? That he could easily put her aside and move on with the future he must embrace for the sake of his country?

Dhalkur would accept his choice of bride but he owed it to his people to choose someone with the skills and background to help him achieve what needed to be done. Someone ready for life as a royal, ideally with some understanding of their language and culture or able to promote his renewal projects.

Not a woman whose prime asset was the fact that he wanted her and she made him feel good. *A woman he cared about.*

His parents had taught him duty and responsibility. To sacrifice personal desires for the greater good. That had been reinforced by the debacle of Fuad's time in power.

Yet for the first time he wondered if the greater good justified the personal sacrifice. Parting from Rosanna *was* a sacrifice. The idea caught him by the throat. The floor shifted beneath his feet and he was glad when Rosanna's terse words fractured his thoughts.

'I see.'

She sat up and shuffled back against the pillows, her breasts jiggling delectably, and Salim's mouth dried. Then she lifted the sheet and tucked it under her arms, something she hadn't done in all the time they'd been here. Salim felt something sharp scrape through his chest and plunge into his belly.

She spoke again, her voice cool and measured. 'You won't be back, will you?'

He stared. Had he *wanted* her to cling and beg him to stay? 'No. It will take some time.'

And their time here was due to end in two days. He had a full schedule lined up after that.

Rosanna nodded. 'You shower while I start packing.'

Salim frowned. He should be glad she was taking this with good grace. That she was being practical.

Instead something like fury ignited. At the negotiators who'd done their job too well. At the foreign king who'd proved ready for a treaty. At Rosanna for not caring that their time was done.

He couldn't imagine driving with her back to the capital. He didn't have enough command of his emotions to act for an extended period as if none of this mattered.

The pain searing his gut was proof it *did* matter. To him at least. Though it wasn't supposed to. Though his lover looked as calm as if he'd commented on the weather, not broken up their affair.

'Don't bother.' He surged to his feet, unable to sit still. He watched her gaze trawl over his bare body and felt a flare of satisfaction at the interest she couldn't hide, but not enough to temper his mood. 'There's no need to pack. Stay the rest of the week as planned and have a holiday. A car will come for you in a couple of days. I'll have a shower and be on my way in ten minutes.'

He turned and strode to the bathroom. Because he knew that even now there was a danger he'd weaken and haul her into his arms.

# CHAPTER THIRTEEN

ROSANNA HAD BEEN back at the capital for four days when she realised something was wrong.

At first she thought she was imagining things. Since the evening Salim had left so abruptly she'd struggled. Every action, every conversation, took so much effort, but nowhere near as much as it took to conceal her hurt.

She'd watched him walk out that night without so much as a farewell kiss and realised she'd made the biggest mistake of her life.

Once she'd assumed that had been trusting Phil, the man who'd duped her. But that paled into insignificance compared with the disaster of falling in love with Salim.

*Totally, irrefutably in love with Salim.*

The man who'd seen her as a convenient sexual partner till their passion ended. Now he presumably expected her to find him the perfect wife.

Not that he'd deigned to see her since she'd returned. She'd tried and failed to schedule an appointment. As if she were an importunate petitioner instead of a valued worker. Or ex-lover.

Rosanna snatched a fractured breath and told herself hearts didn't really break. Yet she grabbed the doorjamb of the office she'd been assigned as she swayed. Her knees had gone soft.

Like her heart and her head.

Because even when Salim had left abruptly, even when he'd thanked her formally for their time together, she'd waited for him to add something. A promise of time together back in the capital, for after all they'd only had five of their seven days. Or some sign that their intimacy had been special to him.

She'd waited in vain.

Five days with Salim had enmeshed her deeper in her feelings for him, while it appeared that he'd been cured of his desire for her. Just as he'd predicted.

Their time together had ended his desire but nearly destroyed her.

That's how she felt, lost and hurting. Unable to work because Salim didn't have time to see her. And because she didn't have the heart to find more possible brides.

Now, on top of that, something else was wrong.

The palace employee who'd just brought her afternoon coffee and pastry, a woman she knew and usually enjoyed chatting with, had blushed and stammered when Rosanna spoke to her. She hadn't met Rosanna's eyes and had scurried away so fast Rosanna wondered if she'd offended her.

This morning something similar had happened with another staff member. She'd wondered if word had leaked out about her affair with Salim. She'd sought out Taqi and asked if she'd done something wrong but he'd refuted the idea.

She firmed her lips. She might be in limbo waiting for Salim to see her, but she could at least get to the bottom of this mystery. Ignoring the tantalising scent of coffee wafting from the tray on her desk, she left her office. Taqi *must* know what was going on.

Moments later Rosanna pulled up short at the large waiting room outside the sheikh's offices.

There on the other side of the room was one of the secretaries who worked with Taqi. Walking beside him in a flowing gown of lustrous amber was Zarah, one of the potential candidates for Salim's attention. The one who, it had turned out, was niece to the Minister for Finance. And there was the Minister, entering the sheikh's office with his niece, a satisfied look on his face.

Rosanna withdrew a couple of steps, putting her hand on the cool decorative wall tiles beside her, needing support.

Salim had halted the matchmaking while he was away with Rosanna. He'd insisted she couldn't resume her work until she spoke to him and he decided how they'd proceed.

Yet here was one of the marriage candidates being ushered, with a member of her family, in to see the sheikh.

Had Salim grown impatient working with Rosanna? Had he decided that, given their intimacy, he couldn't trust her to continue her work?

Obviously he had. He was meeting Zarah without discussing it with Rosanna.

A storm of emotions bombarded her. She told herself not to jump to conclusions. Perhaps Zarah was here for some other reason.

Yet Zarah's work as a photographer wouldn't bring her in contact with Salim. She didn't do portraits. Besides, if they were discussing her work why was her uncle here?

Rosanna recalled the man's antagonism and Salim's comment about him wanting his niece to become queen.

No matter how Rosanna considered it, it seemed Zarah was here for that very reason.

Salim had cut Rosanna out of the process. Maybe it wasn't that he didn't trust her but he felt uncomfortable having her involved now they'd been intimate.

No wonder she hadn't been able to get an appointment!

Rosanna slumped, her shoulder to the wall.

Zarah was graceful and pretty, a local who knew Dhalkur. Who had important family connections. She'd make Salim an excellent wife. She even had gorgeous dark honey-coloured hair courtesy of her foreign mother.

Did Salim find her attractive? Desirable?

Rosanna pressed a palm to her stomach as nausea churned. Nausea and distress.

And an anguished scraping hurt, like claws drawing blood.

*Jealousy.*

She didn't remember stumbling to her room. She didn't remember sitting, staring at the courtyard till darkness closed in. The afternoon was a nightmarish haze, punctuated by the occasional sickening rush of blood when she thought she heard footsteps in the concealed passage to the sheikh's suite. But she'd imagined it. Salim didn't come to her.

Now she faced the truth she'd known for four days yet not quite believed. He would never come to her again.

The realisation made her hollow inside. As if she were nothing but an empty husk.

Except she wasn't completely empty. She still had the capacity to hurt. And to yearn.

Rosanna considered what she knew about Salim.

His pride and determination. He'd needed both to survive life with his sadistic older brother. He hadn't said much about Fuad but the things he'd let slip painted a picture of constant alertness around his brother. And of parents more focused on their royal duties than creating a warm, loving family.

Not that Salim complained. He'd spoken of the valuable lessons learned via military service and royal training and it was clear he'd cared for his parents. Yet his curiosity about her family, his fascination with so much that she took for granted, hinted that his experience of love and even trust were different to hers. Just as his expectations of marriage were completely different.

Yet despite telling herself not to, she'd begun to believe Salim felt more than lust for her.

The trouble was he'd been brought up not to believe in love. He'd made it clear love didn't factor in his world, warning her not to expect too much of him.

That last day when he'd taken her to meet Murad's family and then to his village, Rosanna had been seduced by the heady feeling that Salim shared part of himself. That he really cared for her.

His actions since disproved that.

Rosanna stared at the now moonlit courtyard, the scent of roses rich and heavy in the night air. How many women over the centuries had sat here, pining for a man who would never return their feelings?

For surely the story Salim had told her about the sheikh who fell in love with his chosen bride, and all those generations of descendants who married for love, was no more than a fairy tale.

This wasn't a place where happy ever afters came true.

Even if they did, Rosanna MacIain wasn't the woman

to find one. She'd thought she'd loved Phil, only to discover he wasn't the man she'd believed him to be. Then, despite her caution, she'd fallen for Salim and been rejected.

There wouldn't be a third time. Rosanna refused to open herself up to such hurt again. She was done with love. Or would be as soon as she could take her wounded heart away from here and lick her wounds in private.

She had a horrible feeling it might take years but she *would* get over Salim.

But first they had unfinished business. He'd signed a contract with Marian's company. Rosanna couldn't allow her mistake, agreeing to an affair, to affect that. She knew how much time and money had already been invested in this project and how vital its success was to Marian.

Rosanna would see the job successfully completed no matter what.

The first step was seeing Salim.

All she had to do was find a way to get past all his protective staff and then treat him like a stranger, not the man who'd broken her heart.

Her huff of laughter sounded suspiciously like a groan of pain.

# CHAPTER FOURTEEN

'My apologies, Your Majesty. It won't happen again.'

Salim shook his head. 'One apology was enough, Taqi, and please, stop using my title.' They usually worked informally when alone. 'I've had enough of it for one day.'

The Minister for Finance had been at his most obsequious and had left Salim fuming with frustration. He'd have enjoyed kicking the man out, except his niece, Zarah, didn't deserve such rough treatment. No matter how foul a mood her sheikh was in.

Salim had to give the man credit. He'd known enough to wait until Taqi was away from the office before persuading a less experienced staff member to admit him. Presented with a *fait accompli* it had been easier for Salim to see the pair.

After all, Zarah was one of the candidates Rosanna had selected for him to consider. It made sense to meet her.

Yet it had felt wrong. Even now Salim's gut roiled with distaste. Not at Zarah, who it transpired was a lovely woman, but at the notion of considering a bride.

Because he was still fixated on Rosanna.

He'd avoided seeing her since her return from the Queen's Palace because he needed time to shore up his

defences. He'd had his time with her and now it had to
be over. Though it didn't feel like it.

It felt… No, it *had* to be over. He had a duty to find
the most suitable queen for Dhalkur. He wouldn't dis-
honour Rosanna by continuing their affair while he
shopped for a wife.

'There's something else you need to know,' Taqi said.
'The reason I was out of the office so long.'

Salim looked at his aide and friend and read the
worried furrow on his brow. 'Take a seat and tell me.'

'It's about Ms MacIain. Rumours are circulating at
court about her.'

Silently Salim berated himself. He'd tried to ensure
their affair wouldn't become public but it seemed he
hadn't been able to protect Rosanna as planned.

'It's said she's a criminal. That she and her ex-fiancé
stole huge amounts of money from unsuspecting investors. Some elderly people lost their life savings.'

'What?' Salim braced his hands on his chair. 'That's
nonsense.'

'She told you the truth then?'

'No. This is the first I've heard of it. But I know
Rosanna. She's no thief.'

Taqi gave him a speculative look which he ignored.
Salim knew Rosanna and this simply wasn't true.
'Who's spreading the rumours and what are they using
as evidence?'

His staff had checked her references and qualifications but that was all. He hadn't ordered a full investigation and didn't know all her past.

*Yet he knew her in the ways that mattered.*

Anger seethed through him that people were ma-
ligning her.

'That's what took me a while. I put someone onto

digging into Ms MacIain's past—' Taqi glanced at Salim as if expecting a protest '—while I followed up the source of the rumours. They originated with the Minister for Finance's staff.'

Salim sat back, pondering. The man was a nuisance. Good at his job but always looking to increase his power. His current focus was promoting his niece as a royal bride, not knowing Zarah was already on the list of candidates.

'The rumours began with Ms MacIain's return to the palace. From something a staff member let slip, I suspect the Minister guessed where she spent last week.'

Salim nodded. No doubt he'd made it his business to know. Had he assumed, as Salim had, that theirs would be a short affair, soon over? Rosanna's return to the palace would make him see her as a serious threat to his niece's prospects. That must have prompted his smear campaign.

'What are they saying?'

'That millions of dollars were stolen from investors. That she and her fiancé were in it together. He went to prison and she only escaped sentencing because of an unscrupulous lawyer and a legal loophole.'

Pain clamped Salim's skull as he ground his teeth. 'I knew her ex had misled her but not like that.' He'd imagined infidelity.

'He channelled the funds through a joint account they'd set up, which is why she was investigated. But she was cleared of involvement. There was never any question of charges being laid against her. She lost money too, and though I still need to check this, it seems she tried to pay back some money to a couple of elderly victims, even though she wasn't to blame.'

That sounded foolhardy but noble and all too possible. For all her professionalism he suspected Rosanna had a soft heart.

'Does she know about the rumours?' he asked.

He had to squash them before she found out. The idea of her suffering for what her ex had done, and because of her involvement with Salim, was unbearable.

'I'm not sure. She wanted to see me this afternoon but I've been too busy.'

Salim nodded, his thoughts racing. 'We need to deal with this. Straight away.'

Rosanna surveyed her wardrobe.

She needed something elegant enough for the gala gallery opening and eye-catching because she refused to let Salim ignore her any longer. But she refused to spend her hard-earned money on new clothes just to confront *him*.

Emotions churned but she told herself it was impatience she felt. And determination. Not hurt or regret.

She reached for a scarlet top and a pair of silky white palazzo pants that she'd packed at the last moment. The top had a straight boat neck and its long chiffon sleeves gave an air of elegance. It was perfect, demure because it covered her totally, yet provocative with its unmissable colour and the way it moulded her body.

She'd had enough of fading into the background at Salim's convenience.

What she'd say when she saw him, she had yet to decide. A public event wasn't ideal, but if it was the only way she could see him, she'd make it work.

Rosanna had an invitation to the event because she'd originally planned to introduce some potential brides today. Before Salim decided to postpone her work.

Rosanna's heart lurched. The search was continuing without her.

She hated the idea of continuing the role of matchmaker but she'd despise herself if she let him dismiss her both personally and professionally without making a stand.

The event was crowded. There were locals in traditional clothes, foreigners in suits and designer fashions and enough jewels to dazzle the unwary.

Rosanna ignored them all as she made her way towards the central atrium where the crowd was thickest. Soon she was rewarded with the sight of Salim, half a head taller than most of the men around him and more compelling than any of the art on the walls.

Her heart stuttered and she pressed her hand to her breastbone.

This wouldn't do. She wasn't even close yet she felt a flurry of nerves.

Determined, Rosanna forged a path towards him. Finally she was close enough to hear the deep burr of his voice, and feel it like the memory of a caress stroking her abdomen, breasts and lips.

Despair assailed her.

She couldn't do this. Couldn't march up to him and demand a meeting. She'd done it before but that was when she hadn't known the truth of her feelings for Salim. To face him before all these curious eyes and pretend she felt nothing...

Rosanna was turning away when a voice stopped her.

'Ah, there she is. Ms MacIain, the very woman.'

What was he playing at? He'd avoided her for days yet now he singled her out in this crowd.

She swung around, her breath shallow as that dark, impenetrable gaze snared hers.

Something pulsed between them. Recognition, memory, desire.

No! She might feel that but she had to stop imagining he did too. What for her had been a primal connection had been for Salim simple lust, now eradicated.

'Your Majesty.' As the crowd parted she sank into a deep curtsey.

'This is very timely,' Salim said, beckoning her as she rose. 'My friend here was just mentioning you.'

Rosanna approached, her heart sinking as she recognised Zarah and her uncle with Salim.

'Mentioning me?'

She couldn't imagine why and, seeing the discomfort on Zarah's face, suspected something unpleasant.

Salim nodded. 'The Minister has taken an interest in you and especially your relationship with your ex-fiancé.'

At his words Rosanna froze in horror. She felt again that terrible plunging sensation, as if her stomach went into freefall. Once, back in Australia, she'd felt that way all the time.

'I was about to enlighten him about the actual situation but since you're here perhaps you'd care to.'

*Salim* knew about Phil? She hadn't told him any details. It was a part of her life she preferred not to remember.

Yet as she stood gaping she registered the tension in the small group before her and the martial light in Salim's eyes. Yes, he knew about Phil. The question was whether he knew the truth. Was that anger directed at her?

Suddenly she realised how quiet it was. Conversations around them petered out as people leaned closer. Heat flushed her cheeks as she realised it wasn't only the Minister for Finance who'd heard something of her past.

Taking a deep breath, she said slowly and clearly, 'I was once engaged but I broke it off. I discovered the man I'd trusted was a thief and embezzler. He's now in prison and I have no contact with him.'

The minister frowned, still looking supercilious. 'I'm surprised you weren't implicated too, given your close relationship. Wasn't it true that you were questioned by the police?'

Rosanna swallowed down the sour taste on her tongue. She read malice in his stare and knew he was deliberately making trouble.

But before she could respond Salim spoke, his deep voice carrying. 'Since you're so interested, I can tell you the police investigation discounted that possibility completely. There was never any question that Ms MacIain was involved. She was a victim too. To suggest otherwise is slander.'

Rosanna suppressed a gasp. She wished she'd had such powerful allies at the time when there'd been speculation about her involvement.

'Of course, Your Majesty. Forgive me.' The man gave a half-bow. 'I'm naturally concerned that anyone working in the palace is entirely trustworthy.'

He turned to Rosanna, his mouth tight. She hadn't liked him the first time they met. Now his stare made her shudder. 'It's strange you were taken in by him. You work in recruitment. Surely that requires the ability to judge character.'

'It does.' Rosanna held his eyes, her chin lifting. 'I've learned a lot since then. I've learned not to trust too easily and definitely not to let my emotions cloud my judgement. I let a person's actions speak for them, not the lies they tell or insinuations they make.'

You could have heard a pin drop in the silence. But Rosanna refused to back down, despite his scowl. He knew she referred to him as much as to Phil.

Just as she expected another verbal attack, she felt warmth encompass her fingers. She looked down to discover Salim had moved closer, his hand enfolding hers.

Did she imagine a hushed murmur through the crowd?

Her pulse beat hard and fast, pumping heat through her stunned body. She didn't dare look at him but that touch, that reassurance, meant everything.

Rosanna had fought her own battles for so long she wasn't used to having others stand up for her. Her family had been a thousand kilometres away when the debacle with Phil broke. They'd been supportive but she'd faced each day alone.

Salim spoke, his voice cold and carrying. 'That's an important skill. To mistrust plausible, unctuous people who are motivated purely by self-interest rather than the common good.'

Now there was no mistaking the whispered conversations around them. Or the way the minister's face paled.

He'd been assessed and publicly found wanting by his sheikh. No one listening to Salim could be in any doubt that he was referring to the minister.

Stiffly the man bowed and withdrew, taking his niece with him, and Salim turned to the curator standing nearby as if nothing untoward had happened.

Except he kept hold of Rosanna's hand as he introduced her to the curator and others. Nor did he release his hold as they moved through the building, viewing the exhibition.

Rosanna barely spoke, her emotions too close to the surface as she struggled to maintain her poise. But she couldn't miss the way others reacted to the sight of her standing close by Salim, her hand tucked in his.

Surely aligning himself with her complicated everything?

He'd dumped her. He'd also made it clear earlier that he didn't relish the idea of being associated with a woman who brought scandal in her wake. Admittedly he'd been talking about a wife, not a short-term lover, but surely the same principle applied.

Rosanna found herself biting back a slew of questions as they slowly progressed through the building and spoke with what seemed every VIP in attendance.

She might love this man but she found him impossible to understand.

# CHAPTER FIFTEEN

SALIM KEPT HER by his side through the rest of the event, even leading her to his limousine for the return trip to the palace.

Through it all Rosanna's sense of unreality grew stronger and her body more tense as she fought to appear at ease. She wanted to spurn Salim's touch and demand an explanation. She wanted to curl up against his solid shoulder and take her first unfettered breath in days. She wanted…

*She couldn't have what she wanted.*

Even though he'd stood up for her publicly against one of his most influential advisors.

Rosanna's gait was stiff and her heart bruised as Salim ushered her through the palace and into a large sitting room.

When she recognised it she stumbled to a halt.

Her breath shuddered out. Salim's private apartment. Over there was the spot they'd first kissed. Where he'd told her he couldn't think about any other woman because he could only think of her.

Rosanna's gaze slewed to the door on the other side of the room. The door that led deeper into his private realm and to his bedroom. Horrified, she slammed that memory shut and stalked away from his silent presence behind her.

Salim hadn't said a word since they left the exhibition, presumably because they hadn't been alone. But that silence unnerved her.

She swung around to face him when she reached the window. 'Are you going to explain?'

That took him by surprise. His eyes widened and his jaw firmed. Why? *She* hadn't been the one to make a scene. His friend had done that. Then Salim had compounded it, ensuring everyone saw them together as if they were...

'First you refuse to see me. I presume because I'm an embarrassing complication. Then you parade me around as if I'm some prize VIP for everyone to stare at.'

For several seconds Salim said nothing while the atmosphere between them thickened.

'You don't embarrass me. And I find it hard to believe you don't like being stared at.' His gaze trailed down her body, igniting sparks everywhere it touched.

Rosanna's chin hiked up as she planted her hands on her hips. 'I'm covered from neck to ankle.'

He shook his head and moved closer. 'Maybe so, yet I can see every delicious curve of your body.' His voice hit a deep, growly note that she felt in her marrow. 'And that red screams for attention.'

He was right. She'd been desperate for him to notice her. But she didn't understand what was happening. That fed her annoyance.

'So, are you going to explain?'

There it was again, that glint in Salim's eyes that spoke of temper fiercely leashed.

'You think *I* have something to explain?' He paused,

his stare piercing. 'Why didn't you tell me about your lover?'

'*Ex*-lover. And I did, I told you he'd betrayed me.'

'You didn't mention how. You didn't tell me the trouble he'd caused you.'

Rosanna drew in a deep breath. 'It was no one's business but mine. *I'm* the one he hurt, not anyone here.'

'You think that doesn't matter?' Then before she could process that Salim continued. 'And you're wrong. It's now my business since you work closely with me and reside at the palace.'

Abruptly all her indignation seeped away like air from a punctured balloon. She sagged against the window frame, guilt eating at her. 'You're right. I'm sorry. I never thought my past could reflect on you or your administration.'

'You think I'm worried for myself?'

Rosanna couldn't read Salim's expression except she was sure fury was part of it. This really was the end.

'You're going to break the contract, aren't you? You're going to send me away.'

Suddenly she felt overcome. She'd kept her head up through that interminable public event but now her hurt at Salim's rejection and her fears for Marian's business felt like stone after stone being piled on top of her, crushing her into the ground.

'Come.' His voice was brusque. 'Sit. You look done in.'

'No.' She blinked and tried to gather her strength. It didn't help when Salim was kind. That only fed her weakness for him. 'I'd rather stand.'

Rosanna watched his fingers clench at his sides then stretch out as if he deliberately tried to relax. 'You're one obstinate woman, Rosanna.'

He should know. He was the same. It was something they shared.

'It's how I survive,' she murmured.

She'd need every bit of tenacity and determination to get through the ordeal to come. Leaving Dhalkur. Never seeing Salim again. Knowing she'd damaged her aunt's business at a time when Marian needed her help more than ever as she recuperated.

Finding a way to patch up her splintered heart.

Rosanna sucked in a quick breath that sounded horribly like a sob and forced her gaze from his. Yet she felt the phantom touch of his hand on hers as if he still held it. Just as she still smelled that intoxicating scent of virile man mixed with cedar and spice, though it wasn't physically possible when he stood so far away.

How long before those memories faded? Or would they haunt her the rest of her life?

'What was the idea, holding onto me like that in front of everyone?'

She needed something concrete to focus on. Preferably something that made her angry, because the alternative would be to reveal how sad and weak she felt.

Rosanna frowned, remembering the way people had stared while trying to look as if they didn't. Her flesh tightened. 'It was totally unnecessary.'

'Oh, believe me, Rosanna, it was necessary.'

Staring into his midnight eyes she felt a familiar beat of connection. That infuriated her as did the fact he was holding back. 'But people stared, as if you'd done something significant.'

Salim's guarded expression grew even more unreadable and Rosanna felt her eyes grow round. Her nape prickled in premonition. 'It *did* mean something! Are you going to tell me or am I going to be the only person in the dark?'

She folded her arms around her middle, as if that could prevent the hurt building inside. She didn't know what was going on and felt like she was riding an out-of-control roller-coaster.

Salim spread his hands and lifted his shoulders. 'In Dhalkur the sheikh shakes hands with other heads of state. Other than that, in public he would only touch a member of his family.'

Rosanna digested that. Clearly she wasn't a member of his family. She surged forward, closing the distance between them. 'You mean you were putting your *mark* on me?'

She'd *known* that touching him in public, or allowing him to touch her, was wrong. Except it felt so right that she hadn't been able to pull away.

'You can't just reach out and…and…claim me like a chattel!'

'You're right.' Yet he didn't look in the least abashed. 'Would you be less angry if I said I was primarily thinking about the need for comfort?'

Rosanna jerked back. Had she looked so forlorn? She hoped not, but Salim knew her well. He'd probably read her distress. 'I don't need you to comfort me.'

Salim's mouth lifted in a rueful way that twisted her insides into knots. 'Maybe I was the one who needed the connection.'

Salim watched Rosanna's stormy eyes turn blank with shock.

He was shocked too. Admitting to weakness went against his character. Even as a boy he'd avoided it, with Fuad ever ready to pounce on any weak point. Salim had grown into a man who drove himself hard to do his duty and relegate personal feelings to the back of his consciousness.

He didn't *do* personal feelings.

Until Rosanna.

'What do you mean, Salim?'

Her voice wobbled and he felt an answering tremor rip through him, as if the very earth shook beneath their feet.

'It means I didn't care how it looked or what people thought. I saw you hurting and I wanted to comfort you. Because watching you hurt caused me pain too.' He paused. 'And I wanted to protect you.'

That had been a revelation to him, though not a surprise.

'You already protected me. You championed me. You made a government minister look like a snivelling bully.'

'And so he is.'

It had taken all Salim's discipline not to punch the man in his smarmy face. The fact that Salim had already been poleaxed by the sight of Rosanna marching towards him, sexier than ever and sparking with the latent energy of a lit firecracker about to explode, hadn't helped. He'd wanted to hustle her away from all those avid looks and gossiping mouths. But it had been imperative he deal with the rumours first.

Rosanna opened her mouth and shut it again. For such a forthright woman it was a sign of either confusion or superhuman restraint. Salim suddenly found himself nervous, trying to gauge her reaction.

'When did you find out about Phil?'

'That he'd embroiled you in his crimes? Late yesterday.'

'You heard the rumours and believed them.'

Rosanna's downturned mouth was eloquent.

'No. Taqi came to me with news the Minister for Finance and his staff were spreading rumours that you were a criminal who'd escaped justice on a technicality.' He saw her turn pale and hurried on. 'I knew it wasn't true but had my staff dig for any details on the public record ready to refute the rumours.'

'You *knew* it wasn't true?'

When he nodded Rosanna shuffled across to the sofa and collapsed onto it. She looked stunned.

'I had no idea about Phil's crimes,' she murmured. 'Not until everything fell apart.'

'You don't have to tell me.' Salim wanted to know but not if it caused her more pain.

'There's not much to tell. Phil always had expensive tastes but when he changed jobs he started mixing with people who had serious money and liked to spend it. He was on a good wage but nothing to compare. He told me later that he'd taken the money *for us*.'

Her mouth turned down in disgust. 'He wanted a fancy wedding at the most expensive venue. A honeymoon at an ultra-exclusive overseas resort. To buy a prestige apartment. I kept telling him I was happy with what we could afford. We put a percentage of our incomes into a joint account to cover the wedding and save a house deposit but I didn't check the balance. I thought I knew how much there'd be.'

She sighed and looked down at her hands clasped in her lap. 'Meanwhile he developed a taste for high-stakes gambling with his friends. He lost and stole more in hopes of winning enough to hide what he'd stolen.'

'And he got found out.'

Rosanna nodded. 'I'd actually been going to call the

wedding off. Phil had changed so much from the man I knew.'

Salim sank onto the lounge beside her. He longed to pull her close but held back.

'Thank you for believing in me.' Her eyes, dark as a stormy sky, held his. How he longed to see them glitter brilliant with joy. 'I'm sorry to taint you with my past.'

He shook his head. 'It's a storm in a teacup.' Or it would be once he was finished.

'Nevertheless, I appreciate you standing by me.' She paused. 'And it did help when you held my hand. I felt a bit wobbly. Just as well it actually didn't mean anything.' Her gaze darted to his. 'You didn't really mean it about people thinking you'd claimed me.'

Salim reached for her hands. His chest constricted as he felt how unsteady they were. Deliberately he lifted them from her lap and threaded his fingers through hers.

'Everything I said was true. By now half of Dhalkur knows you're the woman I want in my life.'

Her eyes were huge and troubled but she looked too exhausted for outrage. 'You mean, they know I'm your lover?'

'Some will speculate. But I meant they'll see the action as a clear token of my intention to marry you.'

Salim had been wrong about her exhaustion. Rosanna snatched her hands back and shot to her feet in a single move. But he was just as fast. He stood before her, toe to toe, forcing her to look at him.

'Rosanna?'

She looked stricken. Not what he'd intended or hoped for. Salim was used to women eager for his attention. Women who'd jump at the chance to be his bride.

But Rosanna had never been like other women, had she?

Why had he imagined this would be straightforward?

His gut twisted. She couldn't surely reject him?

She shook her head, her lovely dark hair slipping around her shoulders. 'What a mess. How are we going to get out of this?'

Salim's spine stiffened. 'We don't have to get out of it.'

'You mean I just leave quietly and everything eventually dies down?'

How could she even think it? 'Absolutely not.'

Her head jerked up. 'What *are* you saying, Salim?'

Nerves gnawed at Salim's belly. He felt unsure of himself. Unsure of Rosanna.

But he wasn't a man to dither.

'I'm saying we marry.'

'You've got to be kidding! To avoid gossip? Just because you held my hand? That's pretty extreme.'

'Not as extreme as losing you.'

That stopped her rant. Her cheeks flushed and her questioning look scored him to the bone. He grimaced, fully aware of how he'd publicly put himself and his feelings on the line. 'Don't worry, Rosanna. You can always refuse. That's your prerogative.'

'Why are you doing this?'

Salim hauled in a sustaining breath. 'I thought that was obvious. Because I *want* you, Rosanna.'

She backed away a step. 'That's just lust—'

He took a step towards her. His pace was longer than hers and it brought him into her personal space.

'Not just lust. A whole lot more. Things I never expected.' He paused, searching for some sign she felt the same. 'Your happiness matters to me and when you hurt, I hurt. I want to protect you from harm, but I love watching you succeed at whatever you set your mind to. Did you know I find your competence incredibly sexy?'

Given the way she gaped up at him, clearly not. He smiled through taut facial muscles. It was rare that he found Rosanna lost for words.

'I've fallen in love with you, my darling.'

'That's impossible. You don't believe in love.'

'I didn't. I never expected it.' Which was why he'd been slow to understand what was happening to him. 'But there's no other explanation for the way I feel. I want to make you mine for always.'

Yet Rosanna didn't smile or sink into his embrace. Salim fought not to reach for her, knowing he needed her to come willingly, not because she was seduced by passion. Not because he was the sheikh and he commanded it.

'This is crazy talk. You need an aristocratic wife. Someone who understands diplomacy and Dhalkur. Who speaks the language and can be useful. Not a woman with a tainted reputation.' Suddenly she was blinking. 'Not a woman who doesn't understand the culture or politics.' The blinks came faster and his heart hammered against his ribs. 'Not someone who's brunette and only medium height and—'

'My love.' Salim pulled her into his arms and held her tight against him. Was that a sob? She was shaking, her head burrowed against him so he couldn't see her face. 'Does my proposal make you so unhappy?'

'You didn't propose.'

He slid his hands up her arms and stepped back, holding her at arm's length. Her overbright eyes shone misty grey and Salim felt excitement stir.

'Beautiful Rosanna. Will you do me the honour of

marrying me? Will you be mine for the rest of our lives? I promise to be faithful and supportive and to love you always.'

Her mouth crumpled and abruptly his welling satisfaction disappeared. Had he got it wrong? Did she not feel this amazing connection between them?

'Even though your people won't respect you for choosing someone with a past?'

He shook his head. 'I thought I needed a bride who met all those criteria because I never understood what I really needed was a woman I could love. My people will welcome the woman I choose, because she's brave and true as well as beautiful and kind.'

Her arrested expression told him he'd finally got through to her.

'Even though you risk getting a crick in your neck from kissing me?'

Salim's heart gave a great thump of relief. 'I'm willing to risk it.' He swallowed, his mouth as dry as Dhalkur's mighty desert. 'How do you feel about me, Rosanna?'

'You know far too much about seducing a woman until she can't think straight.' Salim grinned. 'You're also too good at giving orders and expecting to get your own way.' She paused. 'You have an important job and I'm scared I'll be a liability.'

'Never. We'll make a perfect team. You can temper my autocratic tendencies and I can teach you everything you need to know about being royal. I predict you'll become one of Dhalkur's most popular queens. You're honest and decent. You're clever and capable. And you're right for *me*.'

That was what mattered.

She blinked up at him. 'You didn't let me finish.'

Salim held his breath. Surely she wouldn't deny him. Surely she cared. He willed it to be so.

'You're proud and obstinate but you're a good man who really cares about people. You have a kind heart and…' Salim felt as if he was stretched on a rack, tortured, as he waited to hear her judgement. 'I don't think I can be happy without you. I love you, Salim.'

He didn't wait for more. He swept her off the ground and into his arms, her words ringing in his ears and his heart overflowing.

'I should have known from the start,' he murmured against her mouth. 'You bewitched me from the first. I couldn't get you out of my head. When you arrived in Dhalkur it seemed like fate.'

'I doubt it. You were angry with me that first night.'

He shook his head as he strode across the room with her in his arms. 'Not angry. Thrilled. Disturbed. Worried. Desperate.'

Her misty smile made his heart turn over. 'I felt the same.'

'Didn't I tell you this was meant to be?' He shouldered the door open and headed down the hall. 'But we'll take this slow. We'll have a long engagement.'

Rosanna nodded. 'That's a good idea. That will give people time to adjust.'

'Exactly. I'll announce it tomorrow. A month from today.'

'A month! That's barely time to organise a dress, let alone a wedding!'

Salim smiled down at her as he carried her over the threshold into the bedroom. 'It's more than enough time when we have a palace full of staff to organise it. Besides, I can't wait any longer.'

His bride-to-be regarded him seriously then slowly nodded. 'In that case we'd better not delay.'

She reached for the top button of his shirt and Salim laughed with pure, exultant joy. He really had found his perfect match.

# EPILOGUE

'YOU LOOK LIKE a fairy princess!'

Rosanna looked from Salim's cousin, Tara, to the full-length mirror.

'I *feel* like one.' She swallowed. 'I can't believe this is happening.'

The reflection before her showed a poised princess wearing cloth of silver, heavily embroidered in more silver, and wearing diamonds at her throat and ears and in a circlet over her unbound hair. Her dress had a dramatic, mediaeval feel with a fitted bodice that gave way, around her hips, to the heavy folds of her full-length, jewel-encrusted skirt. The long sleeves widened from the elbow to reveal linings of exquisite cloth of gold, embroidered with gold thread and studded with rubies.

Rubies to match the simple but beautiful ruby she and Salim had chosen together for her engagement ring.

Rosanna lifted her hand to her throat, feeling her pulse flutter with nerves.

'Believe it, Rosanna. It's happening and I couldn't be happier for you.'

She turned to meet Tara's glowing green eyes. Her soon-to-be cousin, Her Most Royal Highness the Sheikha of Nahrat, resplendent in a gown of green and gold, looked genuinely thrilled.

'I've never seen Salim like this,' Tara went on. 'He's beside himself with pride and nerves.'

'Nerves?'

He'd admitted to nerves on their way to the Queen's Palace the first time, but she'd assumed he was just trying to allay her jitters. Salim took everything in his stride, even winning around his people to accepting his unexpected bride as their new queen.

Far from spending the month of their engagement busy with wedding plans, Salim had taken her around the country, showing her off like a proud fiancé and giving her a chance to get to know her new home.

'Of course, nerves. The man's head over heels in love.' Tara squeezed her hand. 'It's a new and overwhelming concept for a man like him, strong yet sensitive and raised to think only of his duty. Believe me, I know.'

Her smile turned soft and she smoothed her hand over her just discernible baby bump. Rosanna realised she was thinking of her husband, the rather overwhelming yet surprisingly kind sheikh of neighbouring Nahrat.

'Then he'd better get used to it. I'm looking forward to a very long, very happy marriage.'

'I'm glad to hear it.'

That deep voice, husky with emotion, made her swing around.

'Salim!'

He stood in the doorway, the dearest, most handsome man in the world. He too wore silver, with discreet traces of gold edging, as if he'd dressed to match her.

'What are you doing here?'

'You didn't think I was going to make you walk

down the aisle alone, do you, in front of thousands of people and all that press?'

For Rosanna's father was on crutches with a sprained ankle and couldn't accompany her. Rosanna's mother had considered doing so but knew it would lead to her husband hobbling down the aisle on his bad foot too and probably damaging it more.

'Hey, she wouldn't be alone, she has me, remember?' Tara piped up, but there was a smile on her face.

'I remember, cuz.' He bent and gave Tara a swift peck on the cheek. 'But this is all new to Rosanna and I want to make it as easy as possible.'

'But surely that's not the tradition?' Rosanna queried.

Salim turned and the warmth in his expression undid the knot of nerves inside. She could do anything, even marry with the cameras of the world's media turned on her, when Salim looked at her that way.

'We'll make our own traditions.' His voice dropped to that low, raspy note she knew signified profound emotion. 'My sweet love.' He stepped towards her but, instead of embracing her, took her hand and pressed it to his mouth. 'You look wondrous.'

'So do you, my darling.'

He looked as if he were about to say more when there was a burst of sound from the next room.

'What's that?'

Rosanna turned as the noise coalesced into a babble, broken by the sound of barking.

Salim's hand clasped hers. 'I didn't think you'd want to wait till after the ceremony to see them.'

Through the open door streamed her parents, siblings and her little nephews and nieces, all exclaiming. Then she was in her mother's arms and her father's, careful of his crutches. She was passed from one family member to the other, engulfed in familiar banter and loving reassurances until Salim announced it was time for the ceremony.

Finally, she and Salim were alone.

'That was close,' Salim said. 'Layla and Qamar almost sneaked in with your family. My fault, your nephews begged to see them.'

Rosanna grinned, the two pups, named for the night and the moon, were still learning obedience. Qamar, her coat the silvery colour of moonlight, had been one of Salim's engagement gifts and more precious to her than the fabulous heirloom jewels she wore.

She reached up and straightened Salim's collar even though it was already perfectly aligned. Because she needed to touch him and reassure herself that he was real. All this felt too good to be true.

He lifted his hand, drawing his knuckles softly down her cheek, and she sucked in her breath.

'I love you so much, Rosanna.'

'You stole the words from my mouth.'

A slow smile spread across his face. 'We're going to be so happy together.' He paused, giving her a chance to blink back tears of joy.

'I know.'

Then, hand in hand, they walked together towards their beckoning future.

Every Dhalkuri who saw them together that day knew for certain that it was true after all. Tradition had been restored. The Sheikhs of Dhalkur married only for true love.

\* \* \* \* \*

*If you thought*
The Desert King Meets His Match
*was magical, then you'll enjoy
Salim's cousin Tara's story in*
The Sheikh's Marriage Proclamation.

*Also, why not lose yourself in these
other Annie West stories?*

Pregnant with His Majesty's Heir
A Consequence Made in Greece
The Innocent's Protector in Paradise
Claiming His Virgin Princess
One Night with Her Forgotten Husband

*Available now!*

### #4041 THE KING'S CHRISTMAS HEIR
*The Stefanos Legacy*
by Lynne Graham
When Lara rescued Gaetano from a blizzard, she never imagined she'd say "I do" to the man with no memory. Or, when the revelation that he's actually a future king rips their passionate marriage apart, that she'd be expecting a precious secret!

### #4042 CINDERELLA'S SECRET BABY
*Four Weddings and a Baby*
by Dani Collins
Innocent Amelia's encounter with Hunter was unforgettable... and had life-changing consequences! After learning Hunter was engaged, she vowed to raise their daughter alone. But now, Amelia's secret is suddenly, scandalously exposed!

### #4043 CLAIMED BY HER GREEK BOSS
by Kim Lawrence
Playboy CEO Ezio will do anything to save the deal of a lifetime. Even persuade his prim personal assistant, Matilda, to take a six-month assignment in Greece...as his convenient bride!

### #4044 PREGNANT INNOCENT BEHIND THE VEIL
*Scandalous Royal Weddings*
by Michelle Smart
Her whole life, Princess Alessia has put the royal family first, until the night she let her desire for Gabriel reign supreme. Now she's pregnant! And to avoid a scandal, that duty demands a hasty royal wedding...

HPCNMRA0822

## #4045 THEIR DESERT NIGHT OF SCANDAL
*Brothers of the Desert*
by Maya Blake

Twenty-four hours in the desert with Sheikh Tahir is more than Lauren bargained for when she came to ask for his help. Yet their inescapable intimacy empowers Lauren to lay bare the scandalous truth of their shared past—and her still-burning desire for Tahir...

## #4046 AWAKENED BY THE WILD BILLIONAIRE
by Bella Mason

Colliding with a masked stranger at a ball sends shy Emma's pulse skyrocketing. And that's *before* he introduces himself as Alexander Hastings, the CEO with a wild side, which puts him way out of her league! Will Emma step out of the shadows and into the billionaire's penthouse?

## #4047 THE MARRIAGE THAT MADE HER QUEEN
*Behind the Palace Doors...*
by Kali Anthony

To claim her crown, queen-to-be Lise must wed. The man she must turn to is Rafe, the self-made billionaire who once made her believe in love. He'll have to make her believe in it again for passion to be part of their future...

## #4048 STRANDED WITH HIS RUNAWAY BRIDE
by Julieanne Howells

Surrendering her power to a man is unacceptable to Princess Violetta. Even *if* that man sets her alight with a single glance! But when Prince Leo tracks his runaway bride down and they are stranded together, he's not the enemy she first thought...

---

**YOU CAN FIND MORE INFORMATION ON UPCOMING HARLEQUIN TITLES, FREE EXCERPTS AND MORE AT HARLEQUIN.COM.**

HPCNMRB0822

"Emma," Alex said, pinning her against the wall in a spectacularly graffitied alley, the walls an ever-changing work of art, when he could bear it no more. "I have to tell you. I really don't care about seeing the city. I just want to get you back in my bed."

He could barely believe that he wanted to take her back home. Sending her on her way was the smarter plan. But how smart was it really to deny himself? Emma knew the score. This wasn't about feelings or a relationship. It was just sex.

"Give me the weekend. I promise you won't regret it." His voice was low and rough. He could see in her eyes that she knew just how aroused he was, and with his body against hers, she could feel it.

"I want that too," she breathed.

"What I said before still stands. This doesn't change things."

"I know that." She grinned. "I don't want it to."